David Neth

A Christmas Reunion
A Novella

—Small Town Christmas—
Book 1

D. Allen

DN Publishing

This book is a work of fiction. Names, characters, businesses, organizations, places, events, and incidents either are the product of the author's imagination or are used fictitiously. Any resemblance to actual persons, living or dead, events, or locales is entirely coincidental.

A Christmas Reunion
Small Town Christmas, Book 1
Copyright © 2017 by D. Allen
Batavia, NY

www.DavidNethBooks.com

All rights reserved. No portion of this book may be reproduced in any form, except for reasonable quotations for the purpose of reviews, without the author's written permission.

ISBN: 978-1-945336-00-3
Third edition

Subscribe to the author's newsletter for updates and exclusive content:
DavidNethBooks.com/Newsletter

Follow the author at:
www.facebook.com/DavidNethBooks
www.twitter.com/DavidNethBooks
www.instagram.com/dneth13

Also by D. Allen

Montana Beach
Summer Stay

Summer Job

Summer Nights

Small Town Christmas
A Christmas Reunion

A Christmas Charade

A Christmas Spark

Standalone
Snow After Christmas

December 20th
Tracy

As my driver pulls into the airport, I worry that I made the wrong decision about coming home. There's just too much work to do. I'm not even going back to my place in LA since the press tour ended for the new album. I'm flying right from New York to Batavia. Charlie doesn't like it.

"Why don't I just go back to check in on things? I'll meet you back at your mom's place in a couple days," he pleaded last night.

"What am I supposed to tell Mom when I show up without my husband?" I retorted. Mom's always worried that I don't make enough time for family. She says I work too hard.

And now Charlie has refused to talk to me all day. He stayed back at the hotel while I hit the gym this morning and met with my team at the label one last time before the holidays. He took the last few weeks off from work, claiming we'd be able to spend it together. Obviously he didn't pay attention the millions of times I told him that I had to work up until the third week of December.

What's really set him off is where the argument turned last night. Where it *always* turns: kids. He says he doesn't want to be in his sixties when our kids are just graduating high school.

The airport is crowded when Charlie and I enter. Typical of the holiday season, but before we even reach security, a group of girls stops us to get my autograph and take some pictures.

Charlie stands off to the side and flashes me his phone to show the time. No matter where I am I try to make time for anyone who approaches me for a picture. Charlie usually tells me to politely decline if I'm in a rush. He's not a fan of my career. He thinks that I should stop working at this "silly singing thing" and focus on being a mother.

Yeah, like he doesn't enjoy the private jet and the $3 million house this "silly singing thing" pays for. Not to mention his wardrobe of designer suits that he wears to impress his colleagues. I'm sure they know that I'm the real moneymaker in our marriage. That's gotta be a blow to his fragile masculinity.

Just as the last of the girls is snapping a selfie of us on her phone, Charlie grabs my elbow and says, "Honey, we have a flight to catch."

After security we use a special exit that takes us onto the runway to board the private jet. It's equipped with the works—leather seats, kitchenette, TVs, you name it. It's practically a flying house.

"That was rude," I mutter as I take my seat.

"You're the one who is in such a rush to get home." He takes the seat behind me, which I don't question. We haven't really talked since last night's argument—not that we usually do—and emotions are still high.

Hopefully going to my mom's will alleviate some of the tension. Based on previous holidays and family gatherings, I know that as soon as we get to the front door, he'll turn on his charm and act like the proud, doting husband that he has everyone believing he is.

After I told my mom I was coming home for Christmas, she immediately told me about Daisy Doyle's grand idea to throw a holiday class reunion. I guess her married name is Daniels—still got those double Ds. Her husband has to be deaf. Or blind. Or both.

No, Daisy's not the worst person I've met. When you mingle with entitled celebrities and name-droppers, your faith in humanity pretty much goes out the window. Daisy's just…intense sometimes. Or at least she was the last time I saw her ten years ago.

She wants me to sing something at the reunion. I don't even want to go. We'll see. It's supposed to be a pre-Christmas mixer to catch folks who are in town for the holidays. Everyone else probably already has plans for that day, so it's likely to be a dud. Maybe I can talk her out of having me sing.

It's not that I dislike singing. I love it. Obviously, I've made a career out of it. It's just that I've escalated into a different world than everyone else. "Show business." Singing will only shove my success in their faces and further prove that I'm different. That I no longer fit in with the rest of them.

Still, there are a few people I wouldn't mind catching up with. People I haven't seen since graduation. I had a lot of fun in high school. Besides my family, there isn't really anyone from back home that I still talk to, which is a shame.

I look out the window as the plane rises above the city. The lights beneath are beautiful. Mom would likely be trying to take a million pictures. Of course, she would have to ask for someone's help to find her camera app, then she'd complain about the glare from the window. I can't help but smile at that.

I'm anxious to see my mom. Since Dad died, her health has been slipping. Complications from her diabetes and congestive heart failure. My guess is she hasn't been watching her diet like she's supposed to. My sister, Kimmy, checks on her as often as she can, but she's married with two kids of her own. She's busy. I'm busy. So busy I can't even *call* my mother every week. I'm hoping this visit will help with some of that neglect.

The plane lands an hour or so later at the small county

airport just outside the city. If you would've told me as a teenager that I'd be using it with my own private jet, I never would've believed you. But then, I never would've been able to predict any part of my adult life.

The brisk December wind hits me as Charlie and I descend the stairs onto the runway. My hair flies in my face and I don't notice my sister at first as she approaches, but I definitely hear her loud scream when she spots me.

A wide grin stretches across my face. Someone genuinely happy to see me for me, not just my accomplishments? I immediately feel at home. Besides, she's my big sister. Even though I'm extremely busy, I've managed to keep in touch with her through texts and the random tagging on Facebook.

"Oh, I've missed you so much!" she nearly shouts in my ear over the roar of the wind and the plane. She squeezes me as tight as she can in our puffy coats.

"I've missed you too!" I hold her out at arm's length. "You look so good! Did you cut your hair?"

Kimmy might as well be the antithesis of me. She has short-cropped brunette hair, I have long blonde hair—now platinum blonde due to my stylist determining I need a "bold" look. While she's always supported my career, she would never even think of pursuing the same profession. Too much detail on perfection, too much focus on beauty, too much exposure, too much time.

Besides, Kimmy's purpose in life has always been motherhood. Even before she had kids, she was always the more responsible one. The one to sacrifice her free time to make sure I got to class or practice on time. The one who treated our pets as her babies. Being a celebrity doesn't allow for time to start a family. Especially not when you're "Tracy Slater."

Kimmy reaches back and pats her bare neck. "Yeah. Do you think it's too much?"

"No!" I exclaim. "I think you should put a hat on in this weather, but it looks cute!"

My sister and husband exchange polite nods, but her attention returns to me.

Some of the airport staff usher us into the terminal, where Charlie finally speaks up. He goes in for an awkward hug with Kimmy and says, "It's good to see you. You guys should come out to California sometime with the kids."

Yet another reason why we're not ready to have kids. Charlie just doesn't get it.

It's not like we don't have the room for my sister and her family. I would love to have her. It's just not feasible. Besides, what would the kids do at our house? Sure, we have the pool, but I just know Charlie will throw a fit when they start tracking the water inside the house or knocking too much of it out. And all of our "art"? Consider those gone, Chuckie.

My sister must sense my mood and politely smiles at my husband. "Maybe this summer we can meet up with you guys on tour. I know the boys loved it when Trace brought them on stage with the last one."

"Right. Yeah." The mention of my upcoming work obligations causes him to lose interest.

"Do we have everything?" I ask.

Normally my assistant would be on top of moving the schedule along—even if it's a vacation—but I gave her the rest of the year off. I already felt guilty for having her work so late into December. Usually I give her the whole month off, but the label wanted to push Black Friday and pre-Christmas sales, meaning press got bumped closer to the holidays.

"Yeah." Charlie grabs our bags and heads to the door to the parking lot.

Kimmy brings her eyebrows together and I roll my eyes in response.

NOTHING CAN QUITE compare to sitting in my childhood home decorated for Christmas with the fire crackling and the likes of Nat "King" Cole, Dean Martin, and Brenda Lee playing softly in the background. Add my mother's turkey casserole—likely made from leftover Thanksgiving fixings—and you have the perfect evening.

My sister couldn't stay for dinner. Her oldest son was in his first school play: *A Christmas Carol*. I guess he insisted that his parents go to all three showings. My mom went last night. Tonight is the final night, and I would've liked to go, but I didn't even bring it up. I knew Charlie would make a face and grumble the whole time. For someone who claims to want kids, he doesn't have a lot of tolerance for them.

Not to mention I still need to prepare myself to see everyone. Returning to my former high school in one of my camera-ready outfits is not what I want to do. I purposely packed jeans and modest sweaters to help blend in. I'm not here to upstage anyone.

"Has Daisy talked to you yet?" Mom asks as she pulls the casserole out of the oven.

I fuss with the corner of the forest-green placemat. "Sort of. I've e-mailed her a few times. She's mostly talked to Missy since I've been so busy with the album drop and everything."

"Missy?"

"My assistant."

"Oh." Mom nods. She begins dishing out our plates.

"Do you need any help, Mom?" Charlie asks. *Mom?* That's new.

She smiles. "No, dear, I've got it all under control. You two just take a seat."

Charlie sits back with a smug smile on his face.

When Mom joins us at the table, she continues, "You really should give Daisy a call. She's so happy you're back in town for a bit. She says everyone who's coming to the mixer is excited to see you."

"She told everyone I'm coming?" I groan.

"Well yeah, sweetie. They'll be happy to see you. Why are you upset?"

I shrug. "I don't know." I poke around my plate with my fork. It's not worth it to go into how people expect to see "Tracy Slater," the celebrity, when all I want to be while I'm home is just Tracy, the old high school friend.

Charlie doesn't like it when I talk about the two sides of myself. Apparently it's bogus and I'm just fishing for attention. He doesn't get it. Not like he used to. When we first got together, I felt like he knew everything about me. Of course, we only dated while I was on tour and married shortly after it ended. I suppose it was like summer camp. It worked when we made a special effort to see each other, but now that we're married and have two very different careers, it's just not the same.

"I've got her number by the phone. Give her a call. Oh, not tonight, though. She's in charge of the school play."

I give a tight smile. "Of course she is."

"It's a shame we missed the play," Charlie says. He taps his plate with his fork. "This is very good. Thanks for making it."

I look down at my plate and roll my eyes. What an act.

"Oh, I'm glad you like it!" Mom smiles. "The play was cute. Maybe someday soon you two will be going for your kid."

"Mom!"

"That would be nice," Charlie adds.

"Tracy, you're not getting any younger. Trust me, I was older when I had you girls, and there were certainly challenges. Look at me now! I may never get to see grandchildren from you."

"Don't say that!"

She shrugs. "I'm just saying…"

Charlie nods and looks at me.

I bite my lip and look away.

Mom gets up, grabs something from the counter, and hands it to me. It's one of the magazine covers I did. I haven't seen it yet, so it must've just come out.

"Tracy, I think it's great that you're doing so well, and you know how proud I am of you, but look at that. I'm just worried that you won't have any maternal instincts left if you keep things like this up."

I study the cover and try to determine what she's taken offense with. It's not one of my sultrier poses that she usually condemns. I'm actually smiling in this one!

"What is it?" I finally ask.

"Is there even a reason for you to be wearing a top if you're going to show off the girls anyway?" She shoves her hands under her breasts and gives a little shake. Not what I expected from a woman wearing a sweater with kittens in Santa hats.

My top in the picture is cut lower than I'm used to wearing, but it's still pretty modest compared to most magazine covers. Besides, compared to other pop stars, I'm a saint. But based on the look on my mother's face, I look like a whore.

Charlie glances over. "Mmm, you're right. I don't know if I would've approved of that one if I were there."

I glare at him. First of all, he doesn't *approve* of anything I wear. Second, he *was* there, and I'm pretty sure he was drooling at some of the pictures that were taken. I believe he told me later that I don't fix myself up for him like I do for the camera. And yet, he's stumped why we don't have more sex.

I toss the magazine back on the table. "Mom, these covers are all digitally modified."

"And you're okay with that? What if they changed it so you were naked on the cover?"

"Well, they can't do *that*."

"Then why didn't you ask to see the final photos?"

"If I asked to see the final photos for every picture that's taken of me, I'd never get anything else done!"

"I agree with your mother," Charlie cuts in. "You need to be careful about what you're putting out for the world to see. Our future kids will be seeing things like this eventually."

Mom nods.

"Charlie…" I growl between my teeth.

He knows. He knows exactly what circumstances I'm in. He knows how busy I am and how carefully I put together my brand. Showing some cleavage doesn't ruin that. I know what I'm doing. I've been doing it for years. Besides, my children—if I decide to have them—will know how to respect women.

But if he agrees with me, he can't play up to my mother's expectations of being the perfect son-in-law. I know she sees through the ruse sometimes, but other times I can't believe how gullible she is.

My mother's objections to some of my career choices don't bother me. She usually nitpicks the little things, but I know she's proud of the big things. It seems like she takes an ad out in the paper every time I win an award. And to my knowledge, she's never missed one of my performances on TV—thanks to Kimmy showing her how to use the DVR. She's definitely always been cheering me on, even if she has an opinion on some things.

What bothers me is my husband's complete abandonment of support whenever it suits him. Sometimes I wish he would just go away.

MY OLD BEDROOM is now a guest room. The flowery wallpaper remains, as well as the spot by the closet door that I had used as a coloring canvas when I was six. I remember my mother scrubbing at it for a long time, working away the colorful wax. It still stained the paper, leaving an odd salmon color.

It's a small room for a double bed, but without any other furniture besides a dresser and an end table, it works. What I'm not looking forward to is sharing such a tight space with Charlie. At home we have a king size, so I can pretty much put as much space between us as I need. Besides, our work schedules differ so much we barely spend any time together in the same bed.

"You seemed awfully chummy with my mom," I say as I unload my clothes into the dresser.

"And you seemed awfully pissy." He lies against the headboard, his eyes on his phone.

"At least I'm not putting on a show for everyone."

"It's what you do every day. You should be used to it. What did you tell me? There are two versions of you? Which version am I getting now?"

I slam the dresser shut. "Never mind. You obviously don't get it." I try to walk by him and out the door, but he grabs ahold of my arm.

"Hey, come here." He stands and pulls me into a hug. He has my arms pinned to my side, making it impossible to return it. "Just try to lighten up. It is the holidays, after all."

He leans in for a kiss, but I back away.

"Lighten up? I'm not the one ruining everyone's time."

"Really? You're ruining my time."

"Maybe that's your problem, then."

He overturns his hands. "I think you're the one with the problem. What's the matter? You've been short with me ever since we got here. Before that, even."

I cross my arms and glare at him. "Do you really want to do this now?"

"If it's the only time I can get you to open up, then yes. Let's do this now."

I study him, trying to decipher whether he knows what I'm thinking. This relationship has turned hostile in the last year. I've lost an unhealthy amount of weight. His anger has been growing steadily, not to mention his back acne. Add the cost of his dermatologist and expensive zit cream to the tab of his sugar mama.

"This isn't working anymore."

He looks confused. Clearly we're not on the same page. Either that or he's playing dumb to make me look like the bitch. Wouldn't be the first time.

"What are you talking about?" he asks.

"I want a divorce."

"What?"

I shrug. "Or a separation or something. Maybe see a counselor until we figure it out. But for the time being, you and I can't solve our problems on our own."

He shakes his head. "No, we're not separating. I'm not divorcing you."

"Okay, so *I'll* divorce *you*. If I want to end the marriage, there's really nothing you can do about it." That last bit of information came straight from an attorney I've already got on retainer.

"No."

I squint my eyes at him. "No?"

"Little Miss Tracy Slater is going to get over herself and actually think about someone else for a change. It's time you showed me a little respect."

"Respect?" I fight to keep my voice down. "Charlie, you constantly discredit my accomplishments."

He rolls his eyes. "Please, you're not curing cancer."

"And you are?" He's an investment banker. Basically, shifting money around. Back when I met him, he was my reminder than real people have day jobs. That, and the label loved that his company was always willing to sponsor my shows.

"That's enough. Now let's put on a happy smile and go enjoy the holidays with your mother, which you insisted on."

"I never get to see her, Charlie!" I whisper-shout. "None of my family. I think I deserve to spend a week with them for Christmas."

"And what about my family? You don't think I want to see them?"

"We just saw them for Thanksgiving! Not to mention the cruise we went on last summer with your brother, or don't you remember the private yacht you insisted I pay half for?"

"*We* paid half for!"

"That's funny, because I'm pretty sure the cash came out of my account."

"*Our* account."

"You can say that all you want, but I still make more than you, and that's a fact you can't stand."

I'm thrown onto the small bed, his finger in my face.

"Just because you sell yourself out like a cheap whore doesn't mean you can throw it in my face!"

I stare at him, my heart pounding in my chest.

He balls his fist near my face. "And you keep your

mouth shut about this divorce business."

I watch as he leaves, still frozen in place. My heart races. I hate that man. I want him gone. But in this tiny bedroom and with the approaching holiday, I'm trapped.

DECEMBER 20TH
Stephen

❄ ❄ ❄

I find myself at the bar on Jackson Street again tonight. The muse just isn't with me. Hasn't been in a while. Sometimes I wonder if the height of my career—and my life—is behind me. The magic lost.

Three bestselling books and several other critically acclaimed and fan-favorite books have graced my writing career, but the well has run dry. My publisher pesters me every week for something new. I haven't put out a new book in almost two years. Haven't written anything decent in just about six months.

Of course, it doesn't help that whenever I hear from my editor, she's always saying things like, "Can't wait to read what you've cooked up next!" or "If your previous books are any indication, we're all in for a real treat!"

Despite not writing a single thing today, my shoulders are

knotted with stress. I need to unwind. The weight of failure sits heavy on me, making it even harder to finally write the story I intend to.

The bartender is new. His plain white T-shirt almost seems to bring out the baby fat he still has on his cheeks. Despite his recent employment, I've been coming here so frequently lately that he doesn't have to ask what I want. The bottle's at my usual spot before I even sit down.

"Thanks," I say before I take my first sip.

He wipes the bar with a rag. "You went to school here in town, right?"

I nod.

He pulls a flyer from the wall behind the bar and sets it beside me. "This your class?"

It's an announcement for my ten-year class reunion. The preholiday "mixer" is here. They rent out the restaurant part of the bar now and then for private events.

I've seen the flyers. I got the e-mails.

"Yeah, that's me."

"You going?"

I shake my head. "Probably not."

He shrugs. "Could be fun. Compare how well you're doing to how your former classmates are."

I roll my eyes. "I didn't like them in high school. I'm not going to like them now." I push the flyer away. "Remind me to stay away that night."

He pins it back on the wall and lets me have my space for a while. I read the news headlines on the TV above the liquor display.

"Hank tells me you're a writer."

I snort in response. "Sort of."

"Have you written anything recently?"

I shake my head now and sip my drink.

"Writer's block?"

I nod. "More like loss of talent."

He busies himself with dusting the liquor bottles on the shelves behind him. It's a Wednesday. A slow night.

"I wouldn't go that far," he says. "You'll figure something out."

I brush him off. He doesn't know the story. He doesn't know me. He's still young and naïve. Thinks everything will work out in the end. Well I've been to the end. I know that life doesn't always have a happily ever after. Not like the ones I'm known for writing.

It's funny, but if my readers actually knew who the real G.W. Austin was, they likely wouldn't buy my books. Not just because I'm a man, but because I'm a talentless drunk. Nothing like the swoon-worthy men I write about. God, sometimes I hate myself. I'm a sellout.

"What kind of books do you write, anyway?" the newbie asks. If Hank were here, he'd know to leave me the hell alone by now.

I give him the benefit of the doubt and decide to humor him. "Funnily enough, romance. I started out writing mysteries. The ones with the heavy romance backstories took off. My editor said I had a knack for writing about people in love. Once I wrote a straight-up romance, the publisher didn't want anything else from me." I shrug. "It sells."

"So what's the problem, then?"

"There's nothing left."

He can't be much older than twenty-one, twenty-two at most. A kid. He scrunches his face in confusion.

"I'm not writing," I add. "The inspiration is gone. Whatever I come up with sucks. New York's never gonna buy that. The characters are forced, the vocabulary is juvenile. I just can't write a believable romance anymore. Starting from scratch with a new genre will result in my reputation being destroyed. Poof! Gone."

My words are crueler than I intend, but the kid doesn't seem to take offense. Working in a bar will do that to you, I guess.

He places the bottle of whiskey he finished dusting back on the shelf. "You ever been in love yourself? Maybe that's the problem."

I finish off my drink. "Have I ever been in love? Sure. Once." I pull a ten out of my wallet and set it on the bar. This wasn't as relaxing as I thought it'd be. I'm not about to talk about my feelings to the local barkeep. This isn't a fucking romance novel. Then again, a scene like that would probably end up in the crap I've come up with lately. "That was a long time ago, kid. I'll see you around."

The brisk cold air hits me when I walk outside. Burying my hands in my pockets, I set off for the walk back to my house. It's not far. Maybe ten minutes. As I turn the corner onto Main Street, I nearly collide with two women.

"Oh, I'm sorr—Tracy?"

"Steve?" Her face lights up, and she takes me in for a moment before she reaches up for a hug. "How are you?" she says into my shoulder.

I quickly pat her back and pull away. Returning my hands to my pockets, I say, "Good. I didn't know you were home. It's, uh—"

She nods. "Yeah, it's…" There's a smile on her face, but she doesn't seem to know where to look.

Neither do I. Our footprints in the snow and the ice collecting on the edge of the street suddenly have my interest.

This is Tracy. My Tracy. Right in front of me. "It's good to see you."

"Yeah, I just got in tonight. I'm—"

"You staying with your sister?" I interrupt. "Sorry, you go."

She smiles and looks down. "No."

"My house is too crazy with the kids," Kimmy adds. I've almost forgotten she's there.

"Right."

"You still live here in town?" Tracy asks.

As hard as I try, I can't keep the smile from my face. "Yup. Over on Summit."

She nods. "Gotcha. I'm staying with my mother for the holidays. We should catch up sometime before I leave.

Maybe get some coffee or something?"

"Yeah, I'd like that." I hold her gaze for a while. I divert my eyes to the ground and kick the snow off my sneakers on the sidewalk. "Well, I've gotta get going."

"Right. Me too. We're going to grab something to eat. It was good seeing you."

"You too." I look to her sister. "Nice to see you again, Kimmy."

"Steve," she says with a nod.

During my walk home I'm numb for reasons completely unrelated to the weather. That was the one and only Tracy Slater. The source of all the emotion I put into my books—or used to. The love of my life in high school. The girl I tried my hardest to get over. For a while I thought I had. And then she began popping up on TV and the radio, and I couldn't escape her or the perfect life she'd created for herself.

But still, I know I'll have a hard time getting her out of my head. She was my world. Things like that don't just go away. Especially when I have nothing to show for my life. No wife, no girlfriend, no kids. Just me.

I have no intention of catching up with her. It wouldn't do me any good. She's moved on. She's married. She has a life out in California. I'm just a memory to her.

December 21st
Tracy

I'm sitting outside the Tim Horton's on Main Street. I have to talk myself up before I can go inside. Suddenly the apps on my phone require immediate, thorough attention. The low murmur of Christmas music coming from the speakers is the only thing that fills the air.

Daisy wanted to see me "right away" to discuss the possibility of me singing at the mixer. I'm only here to talk her out of it. Well, that's not the only reason. I needed to get out of the house. Mom went to pick up some last-minute gifts, so it was just me and Charlie. At the moment, Daisy is the lesser of two evils.

With a deep breath, I put on my big girl pants and step out into the cold. Inside, Daisy has already claimed a table. She calls my name from across the small café when she sees me and waves her hand in the air. She's wearing a red sweater and jeans. From what I can tell, she's kept in shape. But then, it's only our ten-year reunion. For the most part, everyone still has their youth. Just look at me and how much I'm exploiting it.

I wait in line to grab a cup of tea and head over to Daisy's table. She hugs me like we're old friends, not keeping her voice down at all. Announcing to the world that she's chummy with "Tracy Slater."

It's funny, because the people in the café likely wouldn't believe I am who I am just by looking at me. Or they just plain don't care. I'm not in my stage clothes. I'm not dressed for a photo shoot. I'm dressed for a trip to the coffee shop. In my black peacoat with my hair pulled back, I'm a normal person. That's part of the reason why I needed this trip. To get back in touch with reality.

"Oh my God, so how have you been?" She bends like a pretzel in her seat, legs crossed, leaning on her palm, eyes wide, and ready for any pop star story I might have for her.

"I'm doing okay." I'm not about to name-drop. "Just released the new record, so up until I got in last night, I haven't really had a chance to unwind from the press tour and everything else. I'm ready to just relax."

"I know! You've been all over the place, girl. I *love* the new album. 'Bittersweet Memories' is probably my favorite. And it's great because I can listen to your stuff with the kids in the car." She puts her hand in front of me on the table and sits back. "Oh my God! You *have* to sign something for my niece! I would be *the* best aunt ever! Mine are still too young, but Abby *loves* you!"

I take a sip of my tea. I should've gotten coffee. Black. Better yet, vodka.

"How old is she?"

"Thirteen. You are her favorite. She doesn't believe me when I tell her we were friends in high school."

"Thirteen." I groan. "You couldn't pay me enough to go back to thirteen."

"Ugh, I know! But it's not like you have money trouble." She laughs loudly.

"Luckily, that's all behind us." I sidestep the money comment. "I know a lot of people probably don't even want to come to this reunion because of all the bad memories." If my media training taught me anything, it was how to steer a conversation back to the point of the meeting.

"Right? That's, like, what I'm afraid of. That nobody will show." Another exaggerated groan. "But I've got flyers *everywhere*. People will come. It's just one night! It's not like we have to relive high school all over again! Wouldn't that be the worst? Ugh!" She giggles loudly, and for just a minute, I feel like I really am back in high school.

"Yeah, I'm sure people will come. I'll be there." Guess that decides that, then. "Even if it's only a few people, it'll be more of an intimate gathering than a big party. The real reunion isn't until this summer, right?"

"Oh yeah! I want to do a couple get-togethers. You know, just to try to coincide with everyone's busy schedules.

If you can't make it to one, you can make it to the other. Do you think you'll be coming this summer?"

I grit my teeth. "Oh, I don't know. I'll probably be in the middle of tour. We're still finalizing dates. It really depends on if I have a show and where I am."

"Well that's a bummer." She pulls out a folder and spreads it flat on the table. Slipping a piece of paper from one of the pockets, she pulls out a pen and says, "That's why you need to sing something for this mixer. Give everyone from high school a run for their money, huh?" She laughs in almost that Janice from *Friends* laugh, and I swear it's worse than when I get the high-pitched feedback in my in-ears on tour.

"Yeah, I actually wanted to talk to you about that…"

She doesn't hear me. "So I was thinking we could do a mix at the mixer." Another laugh. God help me. People are staring now, and it has nothing to do with my fame. "I've heard your Christmas EP and it was, *ugh*, beautiful! You have to sing a few things from that! But then I was thinking that people might be getting sick of Christmas songs by now, so you'll need to sing some of your other hits, too. 'Someday' or 'When Will You Be Mine?' or something like that. The big ones, you know?"

"Daisy, I don't really feel comfortable singing at the event."

Her face drops. "Why not?"

"Well, for one, I don't even have my band with me or any of the other equipment we'd need."

She waves a limp hand at me. "That's okay. Maybe just a few a cappella numbers. You could do 'Silent Night' or 'Have Yourself a Merry Little Christmas.' People love those. They're classics. Besides, you've got the voice for it. Of course, we'll have to narrow it down a bit. One or two—"

"That's not…singing is what I do for a living. It's work. I love it, but when I'm meeting up with old friends, I don't want to have to worry about all that. I'm sorry. I'll help in any other way I can, but I don't want to sing."

Daisy lets out an exaggerated breath of air. "Okay. I suppose that's fair. You *are* on vacation, after all. I forget that this isn't home for you anymore."

That hits me harder than I expect it to. This will always be home. But have I been treating it like that? Not really. I've neglected this town and the people in it since I first saw success. Maybe, against all my efforts not to, I've become a diva so far separated from reality that I can't even identify what really matters anymore.

She closes her folder and sits back, cradling her drink. "Well, I pretty much have everything else figured out. You could come early and help set up, but I mostly wanted to talk to you about what you were going to sing."

I cringe. "Sorry."

Another limp wrist wave. "Don't worry about it. It's okay. It's not like I announced it. I just thought it'd be a nice surprise."

Shrugging, I admit, "Yeah, it would've been."

"Who are you most anxious to see?"

"Me? I don't know." I'm not positive what she implies by "anxious." "Everyone, I guess. I don't really talk to people from high school anymore, so it'll be nice to see everyone."

Daisy rolls her eyes. "Stop being polite! Come on, just between girlfriends, who is it?"

I stutter, not coming up with a coherent answer. And side note—girlfriends? Really?

"Okay, so who are you hoping doesn't come? Or comes but clearly still doesn't have their stuff together, know what I'm saying?" She covers her smirk when she takes a sip of her drink.

I can't help but laugh with her. Despite how annoying she can be, Daisy was always nice to me. I guess I don't mind her company now and then. In moderation. At the moment, I'm content with our chitchatting. It makes me feel normal. Enough that I let myself indulge in a little gossip.

"Is Christie Harowski still around?"

Daisy's eyes light up. "Oh my God! You didn't hear?"

"No, what happened to her?"

"Okay, so after high school, you know how Christie had gotten accepted to Cornell and was going on and on about how she was going to get her master's degree and blah blah blah? Well, that never happened. She went, but during the first semester she got pregnant by some frat boy. She came back here to have the baby and got a job at Walmart. Okay fine. She was working, providing for the baby. Cool. But then, *apparently*, she got in with this one guy who...let's just say he ran a side business out of his car—"

"Really?" I'm leaning in on the table.

She holds up her hand. "That's what I heard. One way or another, she ended up hooked on God-only-knows what, let the baby cry while she was hyped up on whatever she took. A neighbor heard and called CPS. The baby went into foster care and she has to have supervised visits."

My mind has officially been blown. She was in the top ten of our class! She had almost a full ride to Cornell! Last time I heard about her, her life was set.

"Damn." I can't hide my smile. It's horrible to get satisfaction off of someone else's misfortune, but she was not a nice person in high school. Karma is real.

"Yup. So even if she does show up, you have nothing to worry about. Actually, you have nothing to worry about with anyone. You're, hands down, *the* most successful person from our class."

I sip my drink, my mood soured a bit. "I don't know if that's true." The conversation has once again slipped back to my lifestyle. Maybe I need to rethink even going to the reunion.

"Tracy, are you kidding me right now? You have—what?—three multiplatinum records, a fourth on the way, and have made millions traveling the world and being this awesome businesswoman. I think you're pretty successful."

"There's more to success than just a career." I turn my attention to the window, watching as the cars navigate the drive-thru in the wet snow that has been smushed to slush.

"Well, you're married, right?"

I nod. "Yeah."

She slaps the table and my eyes jerk back to her, nearly spilling my tea all over myself.

"Oh my God! I just got the *best* idea! We should have everyone bring in old pictures for a photo collage! Yeah, we could get everyone's school photos from the yearbooks throughout the years! Ah! It'll be *so cute!*"

I grin. "Not sure how happy some people will be about that, but yeah, it's a great idea." I know I made some horrible fashion choices back in the day. That's why I have a stylist now.

"Maybe some candids, too. That'd be fun. Gosh, there's probably *so many* pictures of you and Steve Austin. You still talk to him?"

Tucking my hair behind my ear, I say, "Uh, not really. I ran into him last night. Quite literally, actually."

"Shut up! Oh, my heart is breaking! Everyone thought you two would get married!"

"Well, I am married. To someone else. Not Steve." I'm not sure if I'm trying to remind Daisy or myself. "And besides, he's probably got a girlfriend or a wife or something too."

Daisy shakes her head. "I don't think so, Trace. Ugh, you two were *so cute*! What happened?"

I finish off my tea. "Um…just grew apart, I guess. Listen, I've gotta run. It was nice seeing you." I pull on my coat and give her a wave before heading out the door.

Stephen. If he's single, it makes me wonder what he's been up to for the last ten years. Personally, that is. From what I've seen, he's built a good career for himself. But I can't see him. Not on this trip. Not with everything going on with Charlie. Charlie would get the wrong idea about me wanting a divorce. He'd go to the papers, leak some fictional story.

No. My best option is to stay as far away from Stephen Austin as I possibly can.

December 21st
Stephen

❄ ❄ ❄

Each day I wake up and tell myself, "This is it. This is the day you're going to push through any barrier in your way and finally find the inspiration to keep writing." But each day passes and nothing useful ever comes. The longer I let this get in my way, the more I doubt myself not only as a writer but also as a man. Who am I if I'm not an author? What do I offer the world for my time spent on this earth?

A tad dramatic, I know, but that's collateral damage when you're throwing your characters into the worst situations possible. Well, trying to.

The writer's block has taken its toll on my bank account, too. My last royalty check from the publisher came two months ago. It was a substantial amount, but I've still got a mortgage. I've still gotta eat. If this continues, I may need to find myself a part-time job.

The blank computer screen has been taunting me for an hour now. I've managed to balance my checkbook and scour Facebook about five times by now. I decide it's time for a break, even though I know I don't deserve one.

On a whim, I wander down to the basement. Maybe that bartender had a point. Maybe I just need to dig up some memories to try to help me write from personal experiences. I've never worked like that before, so it probably won't help. At this point, though, I'm desperate.

Boxes are stacked on metal racks along the walls to keep them away from the inevitable flooding that happens each spring. It's an old house, and because I'm concerned about even paying the mortgage, I obviously don't have the resources right now to look into fixing the leaks.

I really should move these boxes up to the attic, but I'll take potential water damage over bat feces any day.

The boxes aren't labeled, so I spend some time riffling through old research papers I thought I'd need later or half-finished novels I gave up on. I'll know what exactly I'm looking for when I see it.

Finally I come across the box containing some old photos. It's mostly filled with various mementoes: my old track trophy, my senior yearbook, disposable cameras I've been meaning to get developed. What I'm really after are the handful of photos of me and Tracy. They're tucked under the yearbook to prevent them getting ruined by dust.

Among the standard fare of prom pictures and team

photos are candids. Lots of them. Goofing around on the bus to different track meets, sledding in Centennial Park, our last few days of high school. These were on the few disposables I somehow managed to get developed. Likely something my mother did for my gradation party.

Beside the collection of photos there's a stack of stupid notes she and I would write to each other in school and force our friends to deliver. Nothing that extravagant. Simple "I love you" notes, or Tracy's loopy writing telling me how much she was looking forward to our next date. The drive-in on Silver Lake or bowling at Mancuso's.

I've always banned myself from remembering those days. They're in the past and will never come again. But like I said, I'm desperate. This is my livelihood. If that means tearing open the wound that was my relationship with Tracy, then that's what I'm going to have to do. Alcohol can always numb the pain later.

It's funny, because I still remember vividly the day I met Tracy. It was the first day of high school. "The big school," as my mother called it. I was walking to school and hadn't run into any of my friends yet. Must've been their parents were dropping them off on their first day. Both of mine had to work, and the school wasn't that far.

She was just coming up the hill from the park. Blonde hair pulled back in a ponytail that swung back and forth as she walked. Her thumbs were hooked on the straps of her backpack. So casual. Just simply beautiful.

I don't know what possessed me to approach her, but

thank God I did. Stupidly, I asked if she was walking to school. Sarcastic as always, she hooked an eyebrow and responded, "No."

We both laughed and continued the rest of the way together. We split off by the time we got to school, but before we did she asked if I wanted to walk her back to the park on the way home. That kick-started our routine. We'd wait for each other at the same corner if one of us happened to be running late. By Halloween we were dating, if you can call hand-holding on the way to school and going to each other's houses for dinner as dating. It wasn't until Christmas that I finally got the courage to kiss her. We were inseparable right up until the time she left for Los Angeles.

Well, that might not be true. The end was rough. So rough that ten years later I'm still not over it.

I've had a few girlfriends since high school. Some of them I really liked, too. Of course, none of them had anything on Tracy. And not the Tracy that the world knows—who is impressive in her own right—but the Tracy that I knew. Back before she stepped into the world's limelight, she was always in mine.

That's the kind of stuff I need to use in the book, but it still seems just out of my grasp. Like there's a thin veil between me and the motivation I need, but I can't quite get my hands on it. Not really. My mind just goes blank as soon as I get in front of a blank page. And it's not just the computer screen. I've tried writing on paper and in different working environments. Everything they say you're supposed to do to kick-start the muse. None of it works.

I put the memories away. That's enough for one day. Time to go for a walk and get my mind off of things. Off of her.

Outside, I purposely head in the opposite direction of the high school, even though everything in me wants to walk the same path and wallow in the memories. It's a small town. There are already too many reminders of the past.

It's cold, but not uncomfortable. I've always enjoyed the colder weather. Everything seems quieter and still. Especially when the snow's falling, the world just seems to stop. Of course, being that it's just before Christmas, everybody seems to be in a rush. That's okay, though, because that's just what I'm looking for. A crowd to get lost in.

I check out some of the window displays on Main Street, but my feet keep pushing me forward. Farther down Main Street until I'm two streets over from the one Tracy's mother lives on. Damn, how did I end up here?

I'm standing outside Kimmy's office, so I decide to pop in. We used to be friends in high school, but after Tracy and I split up, our relationship turned cordial and less friendly. Still, I need to know something.

It's a small realty office, and her cubicle is in the back corner. It must be lunchtime because there isn't anyone at the front desk. Kimmy's surprised when I wander back myself and peek my head around the corner.

"Do you have a minute?" I ask.

She's got a bowl of soup in a white Tupperware container in front of her, steam rising from it. She's totally lost in whatever is on her computer and she does a double-take when she spots me.

"What are you doing here? How do you even know where I work?"

"I've seen your name on a few houses. I've been meaning to stop in and say hello."

She holds her soup and leans back in her chair, blowing on a spoonful before eating it. "This doesn't have anything to do with Tracy being in town, does it?"

For a split second I consider my options: lie and play it off like running into her didn't bother me, or tell her the real reason I came here and finally get some answers.

"Why didn't you tell me she was coming home?" Guess I'm going with the truth.

She shrugs. "It's not like you guys have spoken much. With the way you treated her the last time you saw her, I'm surprised she even hugged you."

"That was different."

"Okay, but either way, do you think it's a good idea for you guys to see each other? You really hurt her."

That stings.

"It's been ten years—"

"And apparently your feelings for her haven't changed. Otherwise, you wouldn't be standing here."

"It's not like anything's going to happen." I deflect the question. "She's married, isn't she?"

"Been looking her up on Wikipedia, have we?"

I roll my eyes. "It was everywhere online a few years ago."

"Yes, she's married."

"And she's happy?"

Kimmy turns back to her computer. "Sure."

"Sure? Who is this guy?"

She meets my eyes again. "He's her husband. You're her ex. Leave it at that. No good is going to come from you seeing her."

I let out a deep breath. Kimmy's made up her mind about me. At this point I'm only annoying her. She's not the one I should be talking to anyway. If Tracy's unhappy in her marriage, maybe she has some residual feelings for me too.

Maybe I'm just grasping at straws here, but the way she looked at me when we ran into each other last night reminded me of the way things used to be. Back when we were happy. That, and why else would she want to catch up with an old boyfriend? Again, I could be making too many assumptions, but it gives me hope.

I decide to risk it and take Tracy's street on the way home. Her mother lives in a big old house just across from the park. I make sure to walk on the opposite side of the street. I don't want them to see me if I chicken out.

I try to talk myself up the whole way there. Just ask her out for coffee to catch up. She suggested it last night. That wouldn't be too weird.

The tree by the sidewalk across the street from her house offers the perfect hiding spot for me. Tracy's in the window, but her attention is inside. A smile spreads across her face as two hands come up from behind her and place something on her neck. A chain of some sort, from the way she presses her hand to her chest lightly.

I spent almost my whole high school career in that house. I know the layout of it nearly as well as my own. She's in her old bedroom. The hands were probably her husband's, who she's very much in love with despite any of my fantasies to the contrary. She's moved on and I should too. How many more signs do I need to tell me to do so?

Giving one soft kick to the pile of snow beside the sidewalk, I shove my hands in my pockets and keep walking. I'm not welcome here.

December 22nd
Tracy

Daisy's idea to put together a photo collage for the reunion has inspired me to look through some of my old photos. I have a ton of them. Mom used to like scrapbooking and got me into it for a while, too. Luckily, she kept most of the ones I put together for my graduation party.

"Oh, look how short your hair was!" my mother says as she points to my prom picture with Steve. She's sitting next to me and smiling as I flip through the pages.

Charlie's on the other side of me. "Is that an old boyfriend?"

"Uh, yeah. I dated him all throughout high school." I turn the page quickly to change the subject, but there's several other pictures of me and Steve. Kissing, goofing around after school, me wearing his track hoodie with his last name on the back.

"The future Mrs. Austin" is stenciled on the page in between the photos.

"You guys were pretty serious then, weren't you?" Charlie asks, stopping me from turning the page.

"Oh, they were inseparable in high school!" Mom adds.

I close the scrapbook. "Do you know where the rest of the photos are? Do you still have them?"

My mother nods. "Oh, up in the attic. Charlie, do you mind giving me a hand?"

"Uh, sure." He tosses a suspicious glance my way and then stands to follow my mom up the stairs.

When I'm alone, I finally get the opportunity to study the pictures in peace. I'd forgotten about a lot of them. Memories I threw away along with my feelings for Steve. Truth be told, we had a lot of fun back then. I was really happy.

Mom and Charlie spend awhile up in the attic, and I've gone through three scrapbooks by the time they come down. It's nice to relive the old days once in a while. This trip home seems to be all about nostalgia, so why not indulge in it a little bit more?

"So how did you two break up?" Charlie asks me as I sort through the box they brought down.

I knew he wouldn't let it go. "Oh, you know how high school was. We graduated, went our separate ways. I haven't seen him since I've been back."

"I thought Kimmy mentioned that you two ran into him the other night?" my mother asks.

I glare at her. She can be so oblivious sometimes. "Oh, right."

Charlie's eyes are on me as he sorts through some of the photos. He asks me a few times to point out who each person is, which is more interest in my former life than he's ever really shown before, but I know it's for my mother's sake more than mine.

I fuss with the new locket around my neck as I look through even more photos, setting aside some that I'm willing to part with for Daisy's collage. Charlie wanted to make nice last night by giving me an early Christmas present. He apologized for scaring me the other day.

We went over to Kimmy and Mark's house for dinner, and while Charlie and Mark were busy with the kids, she straight up asked me how things were going. I never told her I asked for a divorce, but I alluded to our problems. She told me I need to at least try with him, so that's what I'm going to do, even though my heart's not in it anymore. I never really accepted his apology, although the fact that I'm wearing his gift is a sign that he's forgiven, I suppose.

This is his usual pattern: do something stupid, buy me something expensive—likely from my account—consider the matter settled, then go on with his life without actually changing his actions.

I know I need to start calling him out on things like this. I have in the past, which resulted in an explosive argument. Most of the time we simply don't see each other enough, so keeping the peace is all that matters. In this case, I don't want to cause an argument in my mother's house and ruin her Christmas.

"Oh, look at this one." Mom passes me a picture of me and Candace, one of my friends who used to do all the musicals with me.

I look at it and smile, remembering the effort we took to sneak into the auditorium early to take naps before rehearsals.

"Who's that?" Charlie asks over my shoulder.

"One of my musical buddies."

"What's her name? You never talk about high school. I'd love to hear more stories."

"That's Candace. She was a year younger than me. It was usually one of us who would get the lead in the school productions."

Charlie raises his eyebrows. I know what he's thinking. That I always get my way and I always need to be the center of attention. But I worked my ass off to get those roles. Memorizing lines, practicing dance moves, taking care of my voice. And I was even happy for Candace when she got the lead over me. It just motivated me to work harder the next time.

"You know, there might be some more of your things in your closet upstairs," Mom says. "I'll be right back."

"Do you need Charlie's help?" I offer, hoping to get rid of him again.

"No, I'll be fine. I'll holler if I need anything." She disappears upstairs again.

"So tell me more about this old boyfriend. How serious was it?"

I sigh. "Charlie, don't do this."

"Don't do what? I'm just curious about the former men in your life. Seems like you two planned on getting married. Why didn't you?"

"I told you: we grew apart."

"I don't know what you're trying to hide. Is that why you asked for a divorce? Are you sleeping with him?"

I toss the pictures on the table and turn to him. I'm not willing to let him bully me like he did the night we arrived.

"You need to trust me."

"You didn't answer the question."

I let out an exasperated sigh. "No, Chuck, I'm not sleeping with him."

That triggers him and he raises his hand to me.

"I swear, if you touch me—"

"You'll what? Huh?" But he lowers his hand.

I stand and race up the stairs. I tell my mother I've found what I'm looking for and that she doesn't need to search anymore. When I return to the living room, Charlie has moved to the kitchen, peering out the window with a beer in his hand.

I gather the few photos I found and stick them in my purse. As I pull on my coat he asks, "Where are you headed?"

"Daisy wants me to drop these off."

"Well how long are you going to be gone?"

"I don't know." I leave before he can say anything else.

AFTER I DROP the photos off at Daisy's and dodge her requests to hang out, I return to the Tim Horton's on Main Street and sit by the window. I need a break. That's what this trip was supposed to be, but once again, the only time I can relax is when I'm by myself.

I'd mentioned Steve to Charlie before. Obviously I didn't divulge many details, but he never asked, either. As possessive as I know he can be, I don't want to talk about Steve anymore. I'm not going to apologize for having a past. Those memories from high school are special, and I'm not going to tarnish or belittle that for my husband's ego.

"Are you waiting for someone?"

I look up and see none other than Steve Austin. "Oh, hi. Uh, no, I'm here by myself. Have a seat."

So formal. That sounded dumb. Why am I nervous? I guess it's just how awkward this is. What's the protocol for attempting to be friends with an ex?

"Looks like we inadvertently made that coffee date." He holds up his cup and chuckles. I offer a tight smile, which immediately kills his laugh.

"Sorry. It's just been a rough day."

"Oh, sorry to hear that," he says. "Anything you wanna talk about?"

I shake my head. "Not really."

He nods and looks out the window as he takes a sip.

"So tell me about how you've been." The awkward silence is killing me.

"I've been all right, I guess. Can't complain. The writing's been paying the bills for the most part. I have my own house, make my own hours. It's nice."

"That's good. I'm happy for you. Sounds like you're doing exactly what you wanted to do."

"Well, it's not perfect, but it works. Not that I should talk. You've obviously done very well for yourself too."

"Not perfect" is just what it is. "Yeah, but my job has its disadvantages too. I guess they all do in some way."

More silence.

"So do you—"

"How lon—"

"Sorry," I say. "You first."

He flashes a smile. "How long are you in town for?"

"Just until next week. I leave a few days after Christmas. I have a gig on New Year's Eve."

"In New York? That's gotta be fun."

"And scary. Remember Mariah's mess-up?"

"But you don't lip-sync."

I shrug. "I know, but with the cold and everything, my voice isn't going to be perfect."

"I'm sure you'll do great. I'll have to make sure to watch."

"Thanks."

He looks out the window, and I consider my options for a good excuse to leave.

"It's awesome how much snow we're getting this year, isn't it? The past couple years have been pretty light. Hard to believe it's Western New York, you know?"

I shrug. "I spent last Christmas in California, so I guess I haven't paid attention. It's pretty, though."

He nods. "Yeah. Makes me want to be outside. Although, I don't think the kids at the park would appreciate it if I joined them on the sledding hill."

I laugh. "No, I don't think so. We used to spend hours out there."

"Yeah. Hey, they just put an ice rink up on the east side. Do you…" He trails off and sips his coffee.

"I haven't gone skating in years. I'd probably fall on my face!"

"I'll help keep you up," he says.

I remember watching him and his family play hockey in the backyard at their annual New Year's Eve party. I wonder if they still have it. Probably not. Traditions like that tend to die off, and Steve's parents are getting older now.

"What do you say? Do you have time to go?" he asks.

"Uh, sure. Why not?" There's no reason Charlie would be all the way on the east side of town. And even if he was, why shouldn't I be able to spend some time with a friend?

Of course, that's assuming Charlie is mature enough to realize two exes can be friends after ten years apart. Besides, a part of me wants Charlie to see me with Steve.

Not to start an argument, but to prove that he can't control me. I can do whatever I want.

MY LEGS WOBBLE as I attempt to make it from the shelter to the ice in my rented skates. I make it halfway before I clutch at Steve's jacket, and he helps steady me.

"Thanks," I mutter.

We approach the edge of the rink and he says, "Take it nice and slow. Get your balance first."

I shuffle down the small ramp to the ice as a kid no older than ten zips by me.

"Stop laughing!" I call to Steve as I step onto the ice.

He bites his bottom lip. "Not laughing."

I roll my eyes with a smile and begin to inch along.

"Do you need a walker, Grandma?"

"You could help me, you know." I push off the wall toward him and sail in his direction. "Ah! I don't know how to stop!"

We collide into one another and fall to the ice. Well, that was bound to happen.

He stands and offers his hand to help me up, laughing the whole time.

"You used to be good at this! I thought walking in all those fancy shoes would help."

With one hand still clutching the sleeve of his jacket, I brush the snow from my jeans. "Stilettos and ice skates aren't the same thing, Stephen."

"Okay, nice and slow, we'll do one lap around the rink." He holds one of my hands and places his other behind my back and we scoot along the edge.

The rink isn't very crowded—perks of a small town. There are a group of girls who skate in circles, chitchatting the whole way, and several younger kids zooming from one end to the other.

"So I talked to Daisy the other day," I tell him. I'm very aware of how close we are, and I need to get my mind off it.

"Daniels?"

I nod. "Yeah, she's putting together the mixer tomorrow. She wanted me to sing."

"Are you?"

"No."

"Oh."

I watch my feet as they shuffle along. This conversation needs to go somewhere. I don't want things to be awkward between me and Steve anymore. It's been ten years.

"She mentioned that you aren't married or anything. How come?"

"I don't know, Tracy."

Message received. He doesn't want to talk about it. I try again. "How's your brother?"

"He's good. Married, two kids. Lives over on Woodrow."

"So you're an uncle?"

"Yeah, a niece and a nephew. I've actually been bringing

them here a lot this winter. They love to skate. Braden, the older one, actually plays hockey."

I can just picture him helping them lace up their skates, making sure they're wearing their hats and gloves. He probably races them from one end of the rink to the other. It brings a smile to my face. And a twinge of jealousy.

"That's nice. I don't really get to see my nephews a lot with work and everything."

"Yeah, that's rough. But you're traveling the world and doing all this awesome stuff."

"Yeah," I say with a sigh.

"What?"

I shrug. "Nothing. It's just that when everyone talks about their lives—their perfectly normal lives—I feel…" I shrug again.

"Are you jealous?"

"Maybe. I don't know. I guess not."

"I mean, I can see it," he says. "Wake up early every day, spend all day working for a paycheck that barely pays for everything, and then you sleep all weekend to make up for it. Man, you're missing out on the glitz and glamour of the lower middle class. So much better than Hollywood."

I chuckle. "Okay, I get it. I've got it made. I shouldn't be whining."

"I'm not saying that. You can feel whatever you want to feel."

We've circled the rink and wind up back at the entrance ramp. He lets go of my hand and scoots a few feet away.

"Okay, now all by yourself." He waves his fingers toward him.

I push off with one foot and collapse to the ice. That makes two.

He laughs as I cling to the ramp to get my footing.

"It's easy. Watch!" a little girl says as she approaches the ramp, her mother standing at the fence. The girl steps on the ice and kicks off. Meanwhile, my feet slide out from under me as I pull myself up on the fence.

Steve gestures to the girl. "See, even she says it's easy."

"Okay, I think I'm done."

He helps me onto the ramp, where I have a better time walking, and promptly returns his hands to his jacket pockets.

I take seat inside the shelter and remove my skates as Steve hobbles off to get us each a cup of hot chocolate. When I pull the skates off, I stretch out my feet and wiggle my toes, letting them breathe in the cold December air.

"This is the best they have," Steve says as he takes a seat next to me.

I warm my hands around the thin cup. Chunks of the cocoa powder float at the top. Not the best cup of hot chocolate I've ever had, but I don't care at this moment. I'm just grateful for the warmth.

"Did you have fun?" he asks.

"I did. Thank you. I've been so stressed out lately that I needed something like this."

"Well, I'm glad I could help."

"You've always had a way of making me feel better."

He offers me a smile and sips his cocoa. "Can I ask you a personal question? And don't feel obligated to answer. I know I'm being nosy."

My palms grow sweaty. "Okay."

"Are you happy?"

"With what?"

He shrugs. "In general."

"I guess so. Why do you ask?"

"I don't know." He takes another sip. "You just seem down. From what I remember in high school, at least. Maybe I'm just reading into it too much."

I take a deep breath. Should I tell him? Do I want to ruin the evening with a woe-is-me story? But then again, he asked. And he has always been easy to talk to.

"Charlie and I have been having…issues, I guess."

"Is everything okay?" he looks worried.

"I don't know. Things just aren't working. I'm not even sure they ever really did. I just feel like he doesn't truly respect me, and he's too stubborn to work on fixing our problems because he's convinced they're all my fault." Wow, way to unload, Tracy.

"Oh, I'm sorry. How long have you guys been married?"

"Not quite two years. Nothing like a Hollywood marriage, right?"

He bites his cheek. "Have you guys tried, I don't know, counseling or something?"

I shake my head. "That would require Charlie to admit there's a problem."

"Ah, I see."

"Yeah. And it's hard because I'm never home, so we don't really see each other a lot. We've just become too different for a marriage to work anymore. We don't want the same things, and it's impossible to compromise."

Steve takes my hand and squeezes. "I'm really sorry to hear that. If you ever need to talk, I'll always listen."

I smile because I know it's true. Steve's always been a great person to talk to.

My phone buzzes loudly on the metal bench. I pull off my gloves to swipe open the phone.

"Who's that?" Steve asks.

"Charlie," I say. "He wants to know when I'll be home." I guess I have no real way to account for the time I've been gone. It doesn't take two hours to drop off some pictures at Daisy's house.

Steve nods. "Then I guess we gotta get going."

Reluctantly, I get up and follow him back to the parking lot. Each step heavier than the next. My body tensing with dread as I get closer to the car. I wish I go anywhere but home.

Ten Years Ago
Stephen

❄ ❄ ❄

As I head toward Tracy's house, I think about our plan for the coming summer after graduation: find a small apartment in Los Angeles to live in while Tracy records her album and I finish my book. I'd still go to school as a backup plan in case it all falls through, but eventually we'd both become wildly successful. By then, we'd probably get married and live our lives at the top of the world—completely different from this quiet little town.

I pass by a man washing his car, another mowing his lawn, a woman tending her garden, and a couple kids racing each other on their bikes.

Ordinary. Boring. Tracy and I have dreams bigger than this.

Of course, it's been two months since Tracy was first

contacted by that talent scout who discovered her YouTube videos, and now I'm questioning our whole plan. It's not that I don't want to go. I just don't want to go yet.

First of all, I've barely begun the research phase of my novel. If I'm going to shop it around to publishers, it needs to be awesome. That means I need time to work on it properly, which means that when I'm not in school, I can't be wasting my time away at a job to pay for our small apartment in LA.

I haven't quite told Tracy this yet, but I'm sure she'll understand. It's not like she's got a recording contract on the table that she needs to sign. It's just a talent scout who may be able to help steer her in the right direction of one. Surely that can wait a year until I'm done with my book.

I wait for the light at the corner where I meet Tracy to walk to school. Classes are done. Graduation is in a week. Meeting at this corner and walking to school together is in the past now. But we've got so many exciting things happening in our future. I can't wait to start it, but I want to get it right the first time. That's why I think we need to wait a bit.

The move is supposed to be in two weeks. My mother is freaking out because she thinks we're too young and too broke to move across the country by ourselves. My father thinks being young and broke is the perfect time to completely flip your life around.

I guess Tracy's parents are apprehensive too, but they're glad she's not going alone. I'm not sure how thrilled her father is that she's moving in with her boyfriend, but he hasn't exactly said anything.

The apartment we found is a small studio. Some of the big stuff has already been shipped down there. Moving from the East Coast to the West Coast is a bigger ordeal than I envisioned. But when we actually go, we'll only have a suitcase full of our clothes. It's terrifying and exciting at the same time.

Of course, that makes it even worse than I'm having second thoughts. Not about moving, but about moving in *two weeks*. I'm still young, I want to find adventure. Party, go places, live life however I want to. Moving to LA seems like I'll be tied down with responsibilities. Adulthood is already looming over our heads, but I don't see why we need to jump into it so quickly.

I cut through the park to get to Tracy's house. I told her I'd stop by on my way to my buddy's grad party. Tracy was invited too, but she's not that thrilled that I hang out with Jared anyway. His party is sure to get crazy, and Tracy wouldn't like being in that environment. She doesn't particularly like Jared, but he and I have been friends since kindergarten. I'm obligated to go.

Tracy's dismantling some more of her bedroom when I head up. Door opened, per Mrs. Slater's requests. According to her, we're "only eighteen" and have the rest of our lives to "have sex."

"Hey." She's crouched on the floor surrounded by various boxes. A pile of papers and trinkets sits next to her.

"What are you doing?" I take a seat at the end of her bed and look over her shoulder.

"Trying to organize my stuff so I don't leave a mess for my mom after we go."

"Gotcha." Now or never. "I was actually hoping to talk to you about that."

"Is this about your car again? We've already booked the plane tickets. Someone else will have to drive your car over, and we'll just have to make do without one until then."

I shake my head. "No, that's not it. Look at me." I reach for her and she takes my hand to help her stand.

My arms slide around her waist. "You know I'm incredibly happy for you—"

"Oh no."

"What?"

"Are you getting cold feet?"

I stammer, "Well…I mean, not cold feet *exactly*, it's just that—"

"Steve, we've already got everything settled!" She pulls away from me and places her hands on her hips.

"I'm not saying I'm not going."

"Good." She turns back to her mess.

"I'm just saying that we should consider not going right now…" I don't meet her eyes, afraid of what I'm going to see. Anger, disappointment—it doesn't matter.

"What do you mean?" Her voice has an edge, but it's even.

I take a deep breath. "Well, let's think about it. You may

very well be recording an album when we get down there. You're not necessarily going to be getting paid for it just yet, meaning *I'm* the one who will have to pay for everything. Not to mention I'll have school, and that won't leave me any time for me to work on my book."

She shrugs and she says in a softer tone, "So maybe you take some time off from writing until I'm making money from music."

I shake my head. "No, I need to keep writing to work on my craft."

"So I'm supposed to put my dream on a shelf so you can work on yours?" The edge is back.

"Then tell me what we're supposed to do!"

"We do exactly what we were going to do! Move to LA. We'll figure it out. Your books are still a dream for you, but singing is something that could very well become a reality for me."

"So you're saying that my goals aren't as important as yours?" My blood is pumping hard now. This is not the way I thought the conversation would go, and I can only imagine what it'll be like in LA when we're locked in that tiny apartment.

"No, that's not what I'm saying. But we need to look at reality here. I have a lead that could turn into a career. I have to see where it goes! Can't you see that?"

I shake my head. "What I see is a selfish little brat who wants the world to stop for her."

She crosses her arms and looks me in the eyes. "Well

if that's the way you feel, then maybe you should just stay here—for good."

"How are you going to do it without me?"

"I'll manage."

I study her. She's serious, I can tell. Ever since the scout first got in touch with her, she's been full steam ahead on this LA move. Nothing is going to stop her. Not even me.

I turn to leave but linger in the doorway, wanting to apologize or say something that will make her reconsider. But I'm too afraid that if I open my mouth, I'll say more things that'll hurt her.

"I don't understand why you can't just be happy for me," she says.

My phone buzzes and I take it out.

"Is that Jared?" she asks. "Don't you have his party?" I open my mouth to reply, but she says, "Go. Drink your problems away."

THE NEXT DAY I try calling Tracy to apologize, but her mother tells me she's not home each time I call. Message received. Still, I shoot her a text to have her call me.

"Hey," she says when she returns my call the following day.

"Hey. I'm sorry about what I said. You're not a brat."

"Don't worry about it. I know you didn't mean it."

"Good." I breathe a sigh of relief.

It's been a long time since I've been nervous with her on the phone.

"So how are we?" I finally ask.

"Well, that depends. What are you doing?"

"You're still moving to LA, aren't you?"

"I have to. I have to see where this thing goes," she says.

"Tracy, there'll be other offers."

"You don't know that."

"Of course I do. You're insanely talented. Someone will want to make an album with you."

"Somebody already does!" she shouts.

"He's just a talent scout."

"That's more than you've got going for you right now."

That stings, and I let my temper get the better of me. "Wow, is that really what you think?"

"Steve, I—" Her voice is softer, but I cut her off.

"No, forget it. I don't even want to go to LA anyway."

"Fine, then don't."

I end the call and throw the phone on my bed. That was not the way I thought it would go.

The next two weeks are spent more or less the same. Arguing about the move, who supports who, and whose dreams are most important at the moment. Then we cool down for a day or two, try to talk it out again, and end up arguing.

"What about long distance?" She suggests during one of our attempts to reach a compromise. It's late and I'm lying in bed. I'm sure she is too. "You could still go to school out here, I could still do my thing over there. We'd see each other—"

"That's stupid." I'm crankier than I normally would be, but it is a stupid idea.

"Why's that?"

"Is that something you really want?"

"Well, no. I just thought—"

"It's not going to work," I say. Neither of us wants something long distance. And with the three-hour time difference, it would only make it worse.

When we hang up that night, I lie in bed and consider our situation even more. This is probably the worst fight we've ever had. Longest, too. For the most part, whatever differences we had in the past could be ignored or resolved quickly. This is different. This is proof that we're heading in two different directions and growing apart.

I hate that. I don't want to lose her. She's my world. I want to spend my life with her, but I don't see how we can possibly do that if we both want different things. We can't even agree on where to live. The feeling that moving to LA is the wrong choice for me just won't go away. The right choice, however, isn't as clear.

It's now the day before the move and I need to make one last attempt to keep her in my life. I haven't packed a single thing because I'm not going. The question is, is she?

Kimmy answers the door when I get to their house. She doesn't look happy.

"Hey," I say bashfully. "Is Tracy here?"

"Yeah." She sits in the doorway with her arms crossed.

"Can I see her?"

"Oh, now you want to see her?"

I look down at the ground.

"You just had to wait until right before her flight to ruin her excitement for this move again, didn't you?"

"Okay, I deserve that. I just need a minute to talk to her and—"

"And what? Apologize? Move to LA with her and resent her for the success that she'll have and you won't? You know, I used to think you were the best thing for her, but these last few weeks have shown that I was wrong about you."

A lump forms in my throat because I know it's true. I ruined everything because I was jealous. I just can't let her go. Not like this.

"Kimmy, it's okay." Tracy emerges from behind her sister. "I want to talk to him too."

"Are you sure?"

Tracy nods, and Kimmy offers another glare in my direction before retreating further into the house.

"I'm sorry," I say before Tracy even has the door closed. "I'm sorry about everything I said and the way I've been acting. I love you and I want to be with you forever."

She takes my hand. "I love you too."

I smile at her and lean down to kiss her, but she pulls away.

"I'm still moving to LA." She hesitates, reading my face.

"And I really hope you consider coming with me."

I should go. No matter what I'm feeling, I know I should go. But I just can't help but think about the time I'll spend at a job instead of doing what *I* love. And then what happens when I'm miserable because of it all? What other nasty things will I say to her out of jealousy that things are happening for her and not for me?

These past two weeks have shown that we're not equipped to handle the next step of our relationship. Kimmy's right. I'm no longer the best thing for her.

And what about everything I'll be missing by jumping into adulthood so fast? Sure, I'll be going to college, but I won't be the typical college student. Dorming, partying, exploring. I know in the end I'll be content with following Tracy and her dream, but if I already feel jealous because of a talent scout, how will I feel when I blame her for everything I would miss out on? I can't do that to her.

I shake my head. "I can't, Trace."

She hugs herself and closes her eyes tight. "Okay," she chokes.

"Just one year, Trace. Please, just stay here for one more year."

"I can't do that. I need to go. If there's even a chance that this opportunity could work out for me, I need to figure that out. I'd be regretting it my whole life if I don't."

I wrap my arms around her and hold her, but she doesn't lean into me.

"Please stay. Don't leave me." I'm crying now but I don't

care. I just know I can't lose her. This is the biggest fight we've ever had and I just want it to be over. I want to go back to being us.

"You need to go," she finally says.

"Tracy, no, don't do this. Please don't do this."

"I can't be with someone who can't support me." She pushes me away from her.

I stare at her, hoping that this is all a dream or that I somehow heard her wrong.

"Just go." She opens the front door and lingers, keeping her eyes on me for a moment before shutting the door and leaving me outside.

December 23rd
Tracy

*N*o turning back now. Charlie and I are crossing the snow-covered street to the bar and restaurant Daisy has rented out for the mixer. One of the best burger places in the area. Since my team never lets me eat a burger anymore, I'm taking advantage of their absence. As Daisy said, I *am* on vacation.

Charlie hooks his arm around my waist as soon as we enter. We both plaster on our camera-ready smiles and pretend that we weren't just arguing in the car ride over here. Apparently I look too frumpy and I'm coming off too strong as a "regular girl." I just wore what I found most comfortable. But if I wore something nicer, he'd have a comment for that too.

It's funny, because he's the biggest reason I came. After Charlie discovered my previous relationship with Steve, I knew

I'd get twenty questions about what happened with us. I'm *not* prepared for that, and I know everyone will be asking about what happened with me and Steve. Besides, Charlie said he wanted to hear more stories about me from high school. If he's trying to take more of an interest in me, I need to meet him halfway.

Daisy greets us at the door and squeals when she sees me, as if we hadn't just had coffee together two days ago.

"Oh, is this your husband?"

"Yeah, this is Charlie." I tilt my head to her. "This is Daisy, the girl I've been telling you about."

"Right! Nice to finally meet you! It's so great to meet Tracy's old friends."

Daisy offers him a dainty hand and mutters to me, "He's cute."

Charlie laughs and says, "You're only saying that because of the gorgeous woman on my arm." He squeezes me and kisses my cheek.

I hold my smile, but in my head I'm thinking, *Who's trying too hard?*

Daisy eats it up with a laugh. "Oh, that's *so sweet*!" Her eyes linger a moment, and then she points across the room to the food table. "Grab a plate and help yourself," she says. She also points out some of the people who have already arrived.

We make our way over to the food table. Burger sliders, a veggie tray, and a huge assortment of Christmas cookies. I grab a plate and fill it with food, making sure to snag a couple gingerbread cookies—my favorite.

Charlie and I take a seat at an empty table. I see him look down at my plate and back up at me. I open my mouth to protest, but someone calls my name.

"Tracy? Hi!"

I turn and see a slender brown woman approach me. She's wearing a black skirt and white blouse. Very classy, as always.

"Candace!" I stand and give her a hug. "I didn't expect to see you here!"

"Oh, well I'm here with my husband, Jamie." She offers a sly smile as she takes a seat next to me. She's got a full plate of food too. Including cookies. Bite me, Charlie.

"Jamie Bogue?" I grin. He was always cast opposite her in the school productions. She hated it then, but obviously he's grown on her.

"Yeah," she says with a defeated tone. A smile creeps across her face. "He actually got a job offer at Bailey Construction right out of high school, so it's not like we ever missed each other. Actually, we first hooked up at prom."

"Oh God, that was so long ago!"

Charlie coughs next to me. It's like night and day on each side of me.

I sit back and wave my hand to him. "This is my husband, Charlie."

He reaches across me and shakes her hand. "Nice to meet you."

"I saw your wedding pictures in *People* magazine," she

says. "They were gorgeous. You guys look very happy."

"Yup, they were great." I cast a sidelong glance to Charlie and pick up one of the gingerbread men from my plate. "So how long have you two been married?"

"Just about six years," Jamie answers for his wife as he walks up and gives me a hug from behind. "Nice to see you again, Trace."

His fingers trail across Candace's shoulders as he takes the seat next to her. Completely contrasting the coldness between me and Charlie, though I can feel his arm possessively on the back of my chair. He doesn't like how many strange people are hugging me. He should be used to it by now. I hug strangers almost daily. Screaming teens, but still the same idea. I guess it doesn't take much to threaten him.

"How have you guys been? You still live in town?"

They nod. "Yeah, actually just down the street from the middle school."

"Oh okay. That's not bad. Nice neighborhood."

"What about you guys?" Candace asks. "How did you meet? I mean, I read the wedding article, but how much of that was fabricated?"

I shrug. "That story was pretty accurate. His company was sponsoring one of my tours and he came to a few of my shows. Between that and meetings, things just happened."

"It was hush-hush at first, obviously," Charlie says. "A lot of sneaking behind security and avoiding paparazzi."

Back when our relationship was exciting. Now that the world knows about us and the excitement from the wedding has worn off, the spark is gone. And not for lack of trying. I've tried to take an interest in his job and make sure that our life isn't centered around me all the time, but whenever it's just the two of us, things just aren't comfortable. Awkward, even.

He reaches for my hand but I'm still clutching my cookie. "It was all worth it, though."

"That's nice that you could still meet someone with what I can only imagine is a crazy work schedule," Candace says.

"Hell, I'm exhausted after a full day of work," Jamie adds. "I don't know what I'm going to do this time next year."

They both turn to each other and giggle.

"What's next year?" I ask.

Candace smiles. "We weren't going to announce anything for a little while, but I'm pregnant."

"That's awesome! Congratulations!" Inside I'm cringing, knowing full well that Charlie is taking notes. Here, one of my peers, someone who's technically a year *younger* than me, is starting a family with her husband. She never mentioned anything about her job. Already I can imagine what's going on in Charlie's mind. Candace is a housewife and I should be too.

Okay, maybe he doesn't think that exactly, but I know he'd be happier if I wasn't the breadwinner.

"Thank you! We're due in the summer, so we have a little bit of time. Things can still go wrong."

"Don't say that," I say. "Everything will be fine, and by next year your Christmas list will have grown for a Jamie Jr."

He's beaming, and I'm so genuinely happy for them. I *do* want children, but something isn't right. Now's not the time. Especially with the way Charlie and I have been dancing around our problems for months. Since his response to my asking for a divorce was anger, I sometimes wonder if I'm never going to be able to experience the happiness I see in other couples.

"Hey, I'm going to go up and get a drink. I'll be right back." I scurry over to the bar, purposely diverting my eyes from my husband.

A glass of red is exactly what I need right now.

Luckily, nobody seems to notice me at my seat in the corner. Must be my "trying too hard" normal look that conceals me.

By the time I've taken one sip from my glass, Charlie's at my side.

"That was pretty rude," he mutters to me.

"I was wondering how long you would let me off my leash."

"Come on, Tracy, it's the holidays. Let's not argue," he mutters against my ear.

I shrug, knowing that his pleads for civility are worthless. "Okay."

"I would like to talk to you later, though. A serious conversation."

Taking another sip, I shake my head. "I'm not ready for kids yet."

"You haven't really given it much thought."

Turning to him, I ball my fists as I try to contain my composure. "Yes, I have. I just released an album. I've got press to finish, a tour to rehearse, and then I'm going to be on the road for the next six months to a year. Do you really think me getting pregnant right now is beneficial to my career? Besides," I say, returning to my wine, "you know where I stand with us. I told you so the other day."

He ignores that last comment. "You're *always* working on an album. You jump from one project to the next. It's never going to be the right time until *you* carve time out of your schedule."

"Why do you even want kids? It's not like we're at a good place right now between us. A baby's not going to fix that."

I have a sneaking feeling about why he's pushing so hard for a kid. He's a money man. He sees our marriage more as an investment at this point than a union of love. Despite his objections, we signed a prenup before we got married. Having a kid would guarantee that he'd be able to collect child support if we got divorced. He'd continue to profit from his investment.

"We'll figure it out. You'll change your mind once we have them."

"Charlie, at this point, I'm not even sure I ever want to have children with you."

Now I've really pissed him off. I half wonder if he's going to try to push me around again tonight. Looks like my evening will be spent watching Lifetime movies by the fire with my mother. I suppose it wouldn't be the worst night I've ever had, but certainly not what I had planned.

He leans in close to my ear. "Tread carefully, because a story about a whore leaving her doting husband would hurt your career more than a baby." With that, he turns and pushes through the crowd on his way out the door.

I enjoy the last few sips of my wine as I try to cool myself down. Mixed emotions roil through me: anger at him for threatening me, fear that he might actually be able to, and guilt for putting him in a position to destroy me.

I can't stay. People will notice that he's gone, and I don't need word getting out that we're having trouble until I'm ready to release a statement. But who am I kidding? It's a small place in a small town. People saw. People will talk.

Downing the contents of my glass, I slip on my coat and head to the exit.

DECEMBER 23RD
Stephen

✻ ✻ ✻

I nearly crash into her as she exits the bar. The door narrowly misses my face and smacks my shoulder instead.

"Oh, sor—Steve! Hi." She zips up her coat and buries her hands in her pockets. The softly falling snow begins to cling to her hair. "Sorry about that. Are you okay?"

The smile comes to my face naturally. "Yeah, I'm fine. It's okay. What are you doing here?"

"The, uh, reunion mixer." She looks around me and down the sidewalk.

I turn to search for what she's looking for but don't see anything. I completely forgot about the mixer. I never intended to go.

"The actual reunion is this summer. Daisy wants to do multiple gatherings. I guess so the big one isn't so awkward."

I nod. "Right. Well, if half of my high school class is in there, I'm going home." I study her a moment and, against my better judgement, ask, "Do you need a ride?"

She steals another look down the sidewalk and then looks me in the eyes. "Sure, yeah."

"I'm parked over on Center." I lead her through Jackson Square. In the summer, local bands play here every week, but now it's empty. The way the wind whips between the buildings, deep snow drifts form in spots. We meander through them as we head to my car, not a word between us.

"Woo!" I exclaim with a shiver after I kick up the heat in my car. "Remember when winters used to be like this all the time? Seems to be warmer and warmer every year. Of course, then we have a season like this."

I notice her lips stretch into a hint of a grin. "Yeah. We used to build ramps at the end of the sledding hill in the park."

"We'd be out there until we were frozen." I shift the car in gear and slowly pull out of the cocoon the wind and snow has wrapped my car in. We ride in silence as I make my way up to Washington Avenue.

Hitting my left blinker, Tracy says, "No, turn right."

"I thought you were staying at your mom's."

"I am, but I'm not ready to go home. Not yet." One of her Christmas songs comes on the radio and she immediately hits the power button. "I'm not in the mood to listen to myself right now," she adds.

"Okay." A million questions flood my mind, but I turn

in the opposite direction of her mom's without a word.

As she directs me, I realize she's taking me to the "rich" part of town. The city's attempt to draw in suburbanites. The houses are all amazing, even without the Christmas lights. Not all of the houses in this neighborhood put up lights, but those that do look extra special this time of year.

"Do you remember when we used to just get in the car and drive to look at all the lights?" she asks. "God, I loved that. It's not the same in California without snow."

I drive slowly past the houses, admiring the combination of lights and other decorations.

"I remember. That was a long time ago."

She glances at me with a hint of guilt in her eyes. Guilt that shouldn't be there. She had every right to end things with us. "I still think about you."

"You do?" There's optimism in my voice, but I'm not sure what exactly she means. I'm not even sure what I want.

"I wonder what would've happened if I had stayed. If we had gotten married. Where we'd be." Shrugging, she fusses with her cuticles.

I'm surprised. Here I am thinking Tracy had become a fantasy of her former self in my mind, but in reality she's the same girl she's been the whole time. I should've known, because in the last few days I haven't noticed anything different about her. She's still the best thing that's ever happened to me, even if it's over.

"Tracy, you did what you had to."

She nods. "I know. And I guess it's worked out for me.

You just have to be careful what you wish for, I guess."

"What do you mean?" I ask. "I thought you loved your job."

"I do, yeah. But it's a sacrifice. Most of the people at the reunion probably are happily married with kids and the same friends they've had their whole lives. Hell, I didn't even know my best friend had gotten married." She shakes her head.

"Tracy, everyone is so proud of what you've done."

"Yeah. And I appreciate that." She takes in a deep breath. "Daisy said the other day that this isn't my home anymore, and I hate that. This is where I'm from and where I belong."

I shrug. "Yeah, but that doesn't mean that if you had stayed everything would be great. I haven't gone anywhere, and I certainly don't have it all together."

"I guess it just makes me wonder what life would've been like if I had gone down a different path."

"Me too." That's all I allow myself to say.

"Yeah, well…" She wipes at her eyes and pretends to be interested in the lights.

I watch her for a moment before I realize I've been quiet too long. I reach over and grab her hand. "I miss you every single day."

Squeezing my hand back, she looks at me. "I miss you too." She offers a sad smile before looking down again. "Now everything's just so complicated."

"So let's make it simple." I put the car in park and take

both of her hands in mine. It's so quiet I can almost hear our heartbeats syncing together.

She offers a hesitant smile, still unsure of what she should do. I lean in and kiss her. Something I wish I had never stopped doing way back then. Finally, I feel her hands on the back of my neck as she pulls me into her, kissing me back.

For a minute, we're seventeen again. Nothing else matters except being together. And for the moment, that's all that fills my thoughts. That is, until I feel her hands press against my chest and our kiss end.

I sit back wondering what she's thinking. I never used to have to wonder. Now things are different. We're adults, not teenagers. We've both got careers, responsibilities. She's got a *husband*.

Oh God, what did I just do?

"I'm—"

"You should take me home," she says over me.

Now I know we're both thinking the same thing. I shift back into gear and head back to her mother's house. My skin prickles with embarrassment and I barely look at her the whole way back to her mom's.

CHRISTMAS EVE
Tracy

My mother hobbles in the snow and ice down the driveway to her car. She's going to breakfast with a group of her friends to exchange gifts. They do it every year on Christmas Eve morning. She's got a paper bag filled with boxes covered in brightly colored wrapping paper. It drags in the snow a bit as she reaches for the door to get in the car, yet she's oblivious to it.

Wrapped in my bathrobe by the kitchen sink, I sip my coffee and watch to make sure she doesn't slip. Funny how roles reverse as you get older.

"You got in late last night." Charlie pours himself a cup of coffee and leans against the counter, scrutinizing me. Likely wondering why I skipped my morning run.

"The party went late."

"Did it?"

After watching my mother safely back out of the driveway, I turn to him. "Yeah. Why?"

He shrugs. "You sure you didn't meet someone there? Maybe that ex of yours?"

I narrow my eyes. "What are you talking about?" My heart flutters and I try to calm myself down. How would he know about the kiss? We were alone.

Setting his coffee mug down, he feigns a laugh. "You know, I didn't think you'd lie about it."

"Excuse me?" I'm disgusted with his brazen attitude.

He slams his fist down on the counter and I jump. "*Don't* lie to me! I saw you! You and that Steve guy went off into the alley to fuck!"

I roll my eyes. "In the alley? Are you kidding me? We weren't—"

His hands squeeze my arms, and he shoves me back against the wall. Coffee spills down my front as my mug falls to the floor. Shards of glass litter the kitchen now.

"How long has it been going on?" Spittle hits my face as he shouts.

"There's nothing—" My head slams against the wall again.

"How long!?"

The sound of my heavy breathing is the only thing that fills the room. I meet his stare but keep my mouth shut, not wanting to spew the venomous words but also trying not to succumb to the mix of fear and anger. This is the life I created for myself.

Finally, he lets me go. I stay pressed against the wall as he casually takes another sip of his coffee.

Regaining my courage, I say with a quiver in my voice, "When we get back home, I'm filing for divorce."

Slowly, he sets his mug down. I know full well that he heard me. I wait in anxious anticipation to see what his reaction is. It shouldn't be news. I told him the last time he touched me like this. This is not the type of wife I'm going to be.

I study him as he moves past me to leave the room. On his way out, he throws his fist into my stomach, and I curl into myself and fall to the floor.

"No, you're not."

THE CHURCH ORGAN plays hymns as everyone gathers for Mass. I've kept my distance from Charlie all day, and my skin crawls as he wraps his arm around me and smiles like everything is okay. Like he didn't just sucker-punch me in the stomach this morning. But my mother's here and everyone I grew up with, so I put on my own fake smile and take the seat between her and my husband.

My phone buzzes in my coat pocket. It's a text from Kimmy. *Can you come out and help? I've got donations for the church and the boys aren't cooperating.*

"Kimmy needs help. I'll be right back." I'm up and out

of the pew before either of them can protest. I'm relieved to be away from Charlie but feel guilty for leaving my mother with him. But then, church is her social club. He's more likely to feel uncomfortable than she is.

It isn't until the late December cold hits me that I realize I've left my coat in the pew. Maybe a sleeveless dress wasn't the best option for Christmas Eve Mass.

Jaden and Micah run up to me, shouting, "Aunt Tracy!" I just saw them a few days ago, but they're bouncing off the walls now. Likely because they know going to church is the first part of our Christmas traditions.

"Boys, a little help?" Kimmy calls from the car. The back hatch is open, and she's loading wrapped boxes into her arms. Likely clothing that the boys have grown out of.

I give her a quick hug. "Where's Mark?"

"Working. He'll be done in time for dinner, though." She notices my bare arms. "Aren't you cold?"

With a shiver, I nod. "Very. How much do you have?"

"Just these three—Jaden! Watch where you're going!"

I grab a box and shuffle back to the church with my sister and the kids in tow. When we get in the warmth of the church, I ask, "Where are these going?"

Kimmy's still calling to her kids, who are playing in the snow. When she finally gets both boys to come inside, Steve is right behind her.

"You need any help?" he asks.

Kimmy looks at Steve and then me.

"Mom and Charlie already have seats," I say. "Steve and

I can take these back."

"Just put them in the rectory office." She passes off her boxes to him.

I lead Steve back to the rectory. The room is dark and empty, but there are a number of boxes stacked on the floor by the office Christmas tree.

"Thanks." I try to sneak out, but he catches my arm.

"You're freezing."

"I forgot my coat."

"Come here." He rubs my arms. Slowly, I feel the chill leave my body.

I pull away. "No, stop." Noticing the crucifix above the door, I feel the Catholic guilt my mother instilled in me. "Especially not here."

"Hey, I know it's scary. We don't know what exactly all this we're feeling means, but we can't let that stop us from being happy, right?" His eyes are hopeful. "I still care a lot about you. You know that." He's holding my hands now, intertwining our fingers together. "And judging from last night—"

"Last night was a mistake," I blurt, pulling my hands away.

The hope is ripped from his eyes. "What?"

"We never should've kissed. It was wrong and can't ever happen again." I know I no longer want to be with Charlie, but that doesn't mean that being with Steve would be any better. There were reasons we broke up in the first place. Before Charlie even came into the picture. Suddenly being single again is no reason to walk down a road I've already traveled.

"Tracy, but what about—"

"Please don't."

He backs away, hurt. Why am I always doing this to him? Swallowing the lump in his throat, he nods without a word.

I look down, suddenly unable to meet his eyes. Too much is happening at once. I just wanted to have a nice Christmas with my family on this trip.

Before I exit the room, he turns and asks, "You don't really love him, do you?"

"This isn't about Charlie. It's about you and me. We don't work. This fantasy of yours has to die." I steal another look. That was harsh, but after last night I know he's spent the last ten years waiting for me. He needs to move on. Our lives are too different. Harsh is the only way to get the point across. But still, I wish I hadn't said it.

"What happened to you?" The disgusted look on his face tears right through me. He pushes past me as he heads back to the church.

I SHOULD BE asleep right now, but instead I'm out walking in the cold, halfway to Steve's house. I know my words hurt him, and I need to apologize. I wanted to after Mass, but with the crowd and then shuffling back to Mom's for dinner, I never had the chance. I never saw him leave, so I don't even know who he spent the holidays with. I don't even know if he's home. Still, I have to try.

The stillness of the cold night air after the loud and chaotic family dinner reminds me of the quiet moments alone in my dressing room after a show. The party is over, it's time to relax.

Spending the night with Charlie was out of the question. I locked myself in the second guest bedroom—Kimmy's old room—before he could say anything to the contrary. Sleep alluded me, just like it used to every December 24th. But instead of the childhood anticipation that used to keep me up, I'm replaying the day's events.

It's snowing by the time I reach his house. The glow from the TV is the only thing I can see through the window. The first doorbell ring goes unanswered and so does the second. Instead of ringing a third time, I bang my fist against the door, unwilling to take off my gloves in the cold.

I consider just walking back home and leaving it be. I'm all alone in the cold in the middle of the night. Nobody knows I'm here.

The door swings open, and Steve looks at me with sullen eyes.

I push my way in. "Hi." I have no idea where to start. His place is very much anti-Christmas. No lights, no decorations, no tree. The flashing light from the TV is the only thing offering any visibility other than the streetlight.

"I meant to talk to you after church, but you disappeared on me," I say.

He saunters over to the couch and plops down. "No reason for me to stay, really."

My eyes scan the dark room, looking for something to distract myself from this conversation, but this was the reason I came.

"I'm sorry about what I said in the rectory," I finally say. "Not about it being a mistake, but…I don't know. I just didn't meant to hurt you."

He doesn't say anything. I don't blame him for being upset with me, but I wish he'd say something so we could actually talk. Otherwise, why did I waste my time coming here?

But I linger. Not only because I want to make things okay between us, but also because I need to know something.

"You really think I've changed?" I've been thinking about it all night. I've grown, that much is true, but have I really changed that much? It makes me wonder if what Daisy said at the coffee shop is true. This town isn't my home anymore.

"I was mad," he finally says.

"I know. I'm sorry."

"I wish I hadn't said that. You're amazing. Always have been."

I cross the room and take a seat next to him, still a careful distance between us. "That kiss was…" How do I put it? Bad? It wasn't. Wrong? Yes, but only technically. But what makes me think things with Steve would be any different this time around? Things are *more* complicated than they were back then.

"I was out of line," he says. "You're right. You're married, I need to respect that. I guess I just felt something in that moment, and I didn't want to let it go. Not like I did back then."

I smile and fuss with my fake nails, destroying the expensive manicure. I consider telling him the whole truth about me and Charlie, but wouldn't that only confuse things more? Steve was always easy to talk to, and besides my sister, I haven't told anyone else that I'm having marital problems yet.

"You know, I wrote a few songs about us." That seems safer.

"Really?" He grins now too. "I take it this was before you met your husband?"

I shrug. It wasn't.

"What were they about?"

"I don't know. Young love, as cliché as that sounds." I stifle a smile, thinking of the happy place I would go to when I would write songs like that. Back when I first moved to LA. I'd fill my mind with memories of me and Steve. I haven't allowed myself to go to those places in so long. "We thought we had it all figured out back then."

He nods. "If only it were as simple as we thought."

We're quiet again, and I notice the clock on the wall.

Just after one in the morning. I should probably get going.

"Do you still wonder what would've happened if we'd gotten married?"

I flatten a loose thread on the couch. "I don't know. Maybe."

He considers this. "You know, I bought all your music. Even the first album that was—"

I cringe. My first album was bubblegum, an effort by my label to make me marketable. Still, the image of Steve listening to it brings a smile to my face. I can't picture him listening to teeny-bopper music.

"You deserve all the success you have," he says. "I'm sorry for being jealous back then. My biggest regret is not getting on that plane. I just wish I was still a part of your life."

"Did you ever think our lives would be this complicated?" I ask with a sigh.

"No. It all used to be so simple."

"Yeah."

We're quiet for a while longer and then he asks, "You're happy, right?"

I shrug.

"What does that mean?"

I consider lying, but what would that do? He specifically asked about the state of my marriage. "We're getting divorced."

"You are?" A mixture of confusion and hope crosses his face.

"It's—" I take a deep breath and the pain in my stomach reminds me of this morning. "I don't really want to talk about it." I take one of his hands and run my thumb along his fingers. "You know, I've read every single one of your books. Even the bad ones." I smirk.

"I didn't think you noticed."

"Of course I did. I'm very proud of you."

He pushes a strand of hair out of my face. For a moment I think we're going to kiss again. If I'm being honest, that's what I'm hoping for.

"You should get back," he says. "I'm sure everybody's wondering where you are."

I bite my lip. "Nobody knows I'm here."

"What does that mean?" he asks. "What about your husband?"

"I don't want to think about him right now." I brush my hair out of my face. "I just want this whole mess to go away."

"What mess? Your husband?"

I nod. "I feel like I've made a huge mistake by marrying him." My voice cracks, but I push myself to keep talking. This needs to be said. "He doesn't really love me. Sometimes I wish I could just come back here or for you—" I stop. Too much.

"Me? What about me?"

Too late.

"Tracy, what are you saying?" He sits up and looks me in the eyes. "Do you still picture us together?"

"No," I say reflexively. "I don't know. Sometimes, I guess."

"So what does that mean? Where do we go from here?"

"I don't know!" I nearly shout.

It's quiet again, but I can tell he's breathing heavier. I know my heart is racing too.

"I *am* getting divorced," I finally say, my attention on my hands. "I need that, at least."

"Are you moving home?"

I shake my head. "No. Charlie's not the reason I live in California."

"What if we could go back and fix what we've done in the past?"

This forces me to look up at him. "What?"

"I mean that last time, I let you go to LA by yourself. What if this time I came with you?"

"Are you sure you want to?" Is that something I want? My chest burns and my hands are almost shaking. I try not to think of the idea of having Steve on the West Coast with me. Try, but the thoughts still fill my mind.

"I'd be correcting the mistake I made last time."

I look down again. "Then, uh, maybe you should."

I bite down on my top lip to keep the smile from stretching across my face. One step at a time. I'm still married to Charlie. But to me, my marriage has been dead a long time. Charlie is more like a roommate than a husband. And a part-time one, at that.

But Steve makes me feel…good. Happy. Relaxed.

Confident. There's no one else I'd be so comfortable talking with about my mistakes and regrets in life.

"I'd like that." I can tell he's hiding a smile too.

I lean in and our lips meet, but it's different than the cautious approach from last night. Now things are different. We're not just old lovers finding comfort in each other. We're reuniting after being apart for too long.

Christmas Day
Stephen

The way the bed stirs when she moves tells me that last night wasn't a dream, which immediately brings a smile to my face before I even open my eyes. I squint against the sunlight spilling through the blinds and reach for her as she pulls on her clothes. Wrapping my arm around her stomach, I press her against me.

"Morning." I kiss her. "Merry Christmas."

She pats my interlocked hands on her stomach and says, "This is definitely not the way I thought I'd spend my Christmas morning."

"Oh yeah? Is this better or worse?"

"Better," she says with a giggle. She turns toward me. "Much better."

Taking my face in her hands, she kisses me again and again

in rapid succession. I don't want her to stop.

"I've gotta get home before anyone notices I'm gone."

I knew this was coming. Obviously she wouldn't spend all day here. She came home to spend time with her family. It's Christmas Day. Family day. Still, my spirits drop as she confirms it.

"Five more minutes." I pull her back into the bed and meet her lips. I never should've stopped all those years ago. I never will again.

A laugh escapes her and she pulls away from me. "I wish I could. But it's almost seven. Charlie will probably be up soon, and Kimmy and the boys are coming over at eight. The boys aren't going to want to wait for me to open presents."

"What are you going to tell him?"

She tucks her hair behind her ears and gathers the rest of her clothes. "I don't know yet. Today's not the day, though. I have to give him that much. I can't break his heart on Christmas."

I stifle my smile. I have hope for the future now. Our future. Still, I can't help but fear that the wedding ring on her finger is a bond too strong to break. And why should she turn her life upside down for an old boyfriend? That's just me being selfish. This is her decision. I made my position clear last night.

"What are you doing today?" she asks. "You're not just going to sit around here, are you?"

"No. I'm going to my brother's tonight for dinner and

presents. What about you? Are you going to be okay spending all day with him?"

"I've faked happiness for long enough. I think I can manage one more day. Besides, I'll have my family there to distract me." She kisses me again. "I'll see you as soon as I can."

"Have fun today," I call to her as she heads out the door. I mean it. I want her to have fun. I just wish I was a part of it.

AFTER A SHOWER and a shave, I sit down with a fresh cup of coffee at my desk to begin my daily task of trying to call the muse. Usually I'd take time off for Christmas, but with the crap I've been coming up with lately, I need to work.

Today is different. My attention isn't on the stacks of unsorted papers behind my computer screen or the pile of books beside me that I've been using to look at for inspiration. Today, not even Facebook distracts me.

Today I feel refreshed. Rejuvenated. Alive.

For the first time in years, I feel like myself again. The good version of myself. The kind of man I've been striving to be but haven't quite lived up to.

Today, I write.

With the same enthusiasm millions of kids around the world have this morning as they tear open their gifts, I pour all of my pent-up creativity into my work. Everything seems so simple now.

I write until the sunset flashes in my face. I look at the time. Just after four. Having spent all day in front of the computer screen, my mouth is dry. I reach for my full cup of coffee but it's gone cold. I had maybe three sips of it before I was lost in the creation of my own world.

My back snaps and pops as I stretch. I was going to drive to my brother's, but after spending all day in a chair, I'm going to walk. It's just to the other side of town. A bit of a hike, but nothing I haven't done before.

As I step out into the cold, before I even make it off my doorstep, I see Tracy walking with her head down. Her blonde hair covers her face, but I can tell something is wrong. She doesn't look at me when I call her.

Finally, when she's within a foot of me, she meets my eyes. Her left eye is swollen shut. Her bottom lip—the same one she asked me to bite the night before—is now red and puffy. Dried blood clings just below her nose, though she's cleaned some of it up. Her face glistens with fresh tears.

"What's the matter? What did he do? Are you okay?" I scan the rest of her and gently place my hands on the sides of her arms. My heart is pounding. Any joy I had from a full day of writing is squashed.

She doesn't answer me, only presses herself against me, and I wrap her in a hug. We stand like that for a moment, her crying into my chest, snow collecting on our jackets, until I take her inside.

She doesn't protest when I tell her to sit at the kitchen table. I grab a damp dish towel and dab away the blood from her lip. We're silent as I clean her up, my heart aching as I take in her battered face, her crushed spirit. And on Christmas, of all days.

Curiosity bubbles in me. She was supposed to be with her family all day. When did he have a chance to do this? Was it even Charlie? Did a crazed fan find her and attack her for whatever reason? Why didn't she call the police?

I set the towel down, having cleaned her up as best I can, and take her hands. "Trace, what happened?"

She swallows a lump in her throat. "Kimmy had just taken the boys and my mother back to her house for dinner. There wasn't enough room in the car for me and Charlie, so I suggested we drive ourselves. I wasn't thinking. I should've—"

"Stop." I kiss her hand. "This isn't on you."

"He saw me come in this morning. I thought he was still asleep because he didn't say anything all day, but he saw." She begins to cry again and I pull her to me. I've never seen her this hurt, this upset. Even when I was so callous when we were kids, her spirits never dropped this low. At least, not that I saw. Charlie's abuse must've started way before he physically touched her.

"Has he done this before?"

This stops her and she looks up at me. "What do you mean?"

"Has he hit you before?"

"Oh." Her eyes shift away from mine, and she pulls out of my embrace. "A few times, but—"

"But nothing, Tracy." I'm shaking with anger. She's been married to him for almost two years. *Two years.*

Tracy follows me and pulls at my arm as I put on my jacket. "No, Steve, don't. He won't touch me again. I'm leaving him. It's over. Steve, just stay here. Don't get involved."

I ignore her. She doesn't know what she's saying right now. She's been conditioned to make excuses for a man who takes advantage of her. Never again.

As I reach the door, she shrieks, "NO!" with tears in her eyes. She's hysterical, on her knees sobbing. This is not the Christmas she deserves. It's not the life she deserves. I realize in that moment that a part of her misery is on my hands.

So I shut the door.

Christmas Day
Tracy

My hands shake, and I finally let myself accept the fact that I'm scared—terrified—that Charlie is going to hurt Steve the way he hurt me if he goes over there. That could result in a lawsuit, which would devastate Charlie. Despite what he's done to me, I do still care about him. A thought that makes me sick. I don't want to ruin his life.

And then there's Steve. To him, I'm the one who got away. Only thing is, I never realized that all this time, he's been the one I've been running from with a constant look over my shoulder to see if he notices me running. I've been so consumed with putting distance between us that I failed to realize that the thing I wanted most in the world was to run to him and accept my feelings for him.

Now look at where I've gotten myself. Broken and battered by a man who may very well only be married to me for my money. And I let him. I encouraged it. I wanted to put an end to my daydreams about me and Steve so badly that I married the first man who asked me. I didn't care about love. I just wanted a resolution. Marriage was that for me.

Sometimes it's hard to recognize the woman I've become. The woman who is admired by thousands of adoring fans is not the same woman who sits here bleeding and crying on what's supposed to be the happiest day of the year.

Steve turns back to me and takes my hands. "Okay. I won't go. Not tonight."

I wrap my arms around him and pull him to me. I still don't feel like we're close enough. I just want to get lost in him. Turn back time and relive last night.

"Tracy, we're going to have to tell someone about this."

"Why?" I don't want the attention. My team is already going to lose it when they see my face. I have no idea what kind of story I'm going to come up with to explain it. And the fans will soon wonder why I'm MIA from social media.

"He *beat* you! We can't just let him get away with it. Don't worry about the press."

"I *have* to worry about the press! I don't want them to know." I can see it now, an exclusive interview with Oprah or Barbara Walters about the abuse I endured, as if there aren't a million other women out there who have it worse than me. And why should I talk about it? I don't even want to think about it. I just want it all to go away.

"You don't have to protect him. He doesn't deserve that. Look what he did to you. You don't deserve *this*."

I pull away from him. "My husband is a fucking bastard, okay? Is that what you want to hear?"

He puts up his hands defensively. "Easy. I just want to make sure that he can't ever do this again. That you're going to be able to get away from him without any more pain."

He means well, I know that. I know it's because he still cares for me, but he has to know that this isn't easy for me, either. I don't want to be with Charlie anymore, but that doesn't mean I need to ruin his life on my way out.

Taking hold of my hand, he says, "I think we should go to the police. They're going to need to take photographs in order to—"

I pull away from him and stand up. "I told you no. Drop it."

"Tracy, you don't have to be afraid of him."

"I'm *not* afraid of him! And if you think that's why I don't want to go to the police, then you obviously don't know me very well." I leave the room before he can respond.

I need time to think. Everything's happened so fast, I just want to get away from it all for a moment.

I barricade myself in Stephen's bedroom, lying on his bed and staring at the ceiling, thinking about what a circus sideshow my life has become, rethinking the steps I've taken to get here.

The media is going to eat this up. The label will probably love it because they can milk it for publicity. That's not what my brand is about. I don't want to have to play the victim in order to sell albums.

And even though I just put out an album, I'm sure everyone will be expecting me to write about the destruction of my marriage and my abuse for the next one. As if that's something I want to exploit and relive night after night while I'm on tour.

I'm brooding, I know. *That's* not the type of person I am, either. Steve is probably just as scared as I am and wants to make sure I'm okay. I'm not ready to go to the police just yet. Tomorrow I'll have to. I just need to grow up enough to tell Steve that instead of storming off and pouting.

The door opens slowly, and Steve peeks his head in.

"Hey, can I come in?"

I sit up. "Yeah."

He sits next to me on the bed. "I'm sorry for pushing you. I just hate seeing what he's done to you."

I fuss with my nails. I've already worked off three on my left hand and two on my right. "I know. I'm just not ready yet. You have to respect that."

He lets out a deep breath. "Okay."

I let him pull me back to him. He kisses the top of my head. "I made hot chocolate. It's downstairs. We could just watch a movie and relax."

I breathe a sigh of relief. Finally, the discussion is over and my Christmas can be salvaged. This is what I wanted. A quiet, relaxing evening at home with the people I care most about. I spent all day with my family, now it's Steve's turn.

We go downstairs and he sets up the movie. I wrap myself up in the small throw on the couch. He sits a comfortable distance away, but I snuggle closer to him, and he finally wraps his arm around my shoulders.

We watch in silence. Admittedly, it's the first Christmas movie I've seen this year. With everything going on, I've barely even registered that it was the Christmas season.

The movie ends and I readjust so I'm facing Steve. He's been in my thoughts for the last half hour, blocking out the actual movie from my mind.

"I need to tell you something."

"Okay." He rubs my leg to keep me warm.

My heart pounds and my face burns.

Suddenly I can't look him in the eyes. Whatever courage I had that Charlie didn't squash is focused on getting the words out.

"Charlie and I are over. I understand that we need to tell the police, but not tonight."

"We should do it first thing tomorrow morning, though."

"We will, but that's not what I wanted to tell you." I take a deep breath again, preparing myself to voice what I've recently—very recently—accepted. "I'm still in love with you. I never stopped thinking about you. You were my first love. And, I guess, my only love."

I chance a look up at him and see that he's smiling. I'd be lying if I said I wasn't relieved. I know he still cares for me, that much is obvious. But on some level I know I'll always care about Charlie, too, despite what he's done to me. I always thought that was the way Steve viewed me.

"I love you too."

He kisses me gently but I pull away.

"I feel guilty. Like you should be mad at me."

"Mad at you for what?" he asks.

"You broke my heart back in high school. You paid more attention to starting your writing career than you did to me. And I know, obviously that's worked out for you. I'm very proud of who you've become." I shrug. "I don't know. Maybe that was just a rough patch in our relationship and a couple of eighteen-year-olds didn't know how to handle it."

"Tracy, what are you saying?"

"I'm saying I shouldn't have broken up with you back then. I was being selfish. Now look at us. You're miserable. I'm married to a man who thinks it's okay to hit me. Yet here we both are, together again."

He brushes the hair out of my eyes.

"I think we needed that time apart. We were heading in two different directions then, and they circled back to this moment right here." He takes my hand and kisses the back of it. "If you hadn't broken up with me then, I'd have only held you back and you wouldn't have become the successful musician you are. Eighteen-year-old Steve was too consumed with himself to worry about the dreams of someone else."

"But I hurt you. And then I went and married Charlie, thinking my feelings for you would go away once I had one of these." I hold up my left hand and wiggle my ring finger. It sits heavy on my hand. I pull it off and set it on the table. I don't need it anymore. "Now I'm hurting him too, all because I was too scared to admit how I felt about you. Because I love you. I really do."

The tears begin to flow, and I press my lips to his again. They began as guilty tears, but feeling his touch—more tender and comforting than Charlie's—I know they're happy tears. I've finally found my way home.

"Forget about what happened," he says. "Where do you want to go from here? Not just with us, but everything. What do you want?"

The question hangs in the air as I consider it. What do I want? It's so simple but carries so much weight. I don't even know the answer. Not really.

Lately I feel like I've been going through the motions without enjoying much of anything. My life has become a routine. It's all fun—performing, recording, promoting—but it doesn't have the value it should have for me. Something is holding me back, and I need to figure out what it is. Where I want to go. What I want to do.

December 26th
Stephen

❄ ❄ ❄

The kitchen light blinds me early the next morning. My father used to make breakfast every year on Christmas morning. It's a day late, but I figured it'd be a nice treat for Tracy. She needs helpful surprises right now.

The day after Christmas always used to make me depressed. Everything the month had been working up to was over. The magic gone. The lights were still on but the party had ended. We were only left with the wrapping paper carnage and a refrigerator full of leftovers. It was yet another reminder that nothing lasts forever.

Just like this pancake mix that's been in the pantry forever. Mold is clumping at the bottom. Guess it's French toast today. Not what my Dad used to make, but it'll do.

This year certainly isn't like every other year, anyway.

Christmas didn't live up to its hype. Christmas Day can sometimes bend the rules of time and space. With the fantasy of it all, the hours seem to stretch longer than any other day.

This year surprised me with my whirlwind of feelings. I never used to be this emotional. I rationalize and take things as they come. Maybe that was my issue with my book. I didn't allow myself to invest emotionally into it.

Today is a do-over Christmas. I still woke up next to the woman I love. It can't be *that* bad of a day. The events of yesterday are behind us. It's the first day of the rest of our lives.

She greets me in the kitchen before I finish making our breakfast.

"I thought you'd sleep in longer." I place a full plate in front of her.

"I heard you from upstairs. What's with this?"

"It's our Christmas do-over since yesterday sucked."

She smiles and digs in to her breakfast.

I turn off the stove, pile the rest of the French toast on my plate, and take the seat opposite her. I'm not used to having a breakfast companion.

"I still want to go to the police today," she says.

I'm happy to hear it because I know it's the right thing to do, even if it's not the easiest for her. Her hesitation last night was understandable.

"Will you come with me?"

I look up from my food. "You sure that's a good idea?"

"Why wouldn't it be?"

"It might look suspicious if I come."

"Oh." She considers this a moment and then adds, "They can call me whatever they want. It doesn't excuse what he's done to me."

"Okay, then. I'll come."

We eat in silence for another minute, neither one of us liking this conversation. Necessary, but uncomfortable.

"They're probably going to ask why you didn't come in last night," I finally say.

"It was Christmas and I didn't want the attention. Now that I've had a night's rest, I'm thinking clearer."

She's clearly had some time to think about this. Then again, why wouldn't this be the first thing on her mind? I'm sure she can't help but replay the memories of him hitting her and—

"Have you told your mother yet? Isn't he staying with her?" I need to distract myself from thinking about it. Her face looks better today, but it's still puffy. Good for the police report, bad for her.

"I texted my sister and told her we had a fight. That was it. Mom was at her house last night, though."

"You should call her and tell her. Better yet, go see her."

She shakes her head. "Not right now. Not until after we've gone to the police. She's only going to worry and stress me out. I need to take control of the situation first."

I smile at her strength but look down at my food to hide it. She's certainly come a long way. We both have.

Tracy and I walk into the police station nervously. Neither of us have been in here before, and I can tell the thought of filing a report against her husband is unsettling to her. I don't blame her. Despite her hesitations, she bravely recounts what's happened to the woman at the desk.

They take Tracy into another room, and I sit in a small metal chair by the front door. Nothing on my phone captures my attention enough.

What seems like three hours later, Tracy and an officer emerge from the room. They have her sign some paperwork, but after that she pulls on her coat. "Ready?"

"How'd it go?" I ask her once we're outside.

"Good, I guess," she says with a sigh. "They took pictures, asked me why I never came in yesterday when it happened, like you said they would, and got my official statement."

"So what happens now?"

"We should stop at my mother's. She's going to want to see me."

"What about Charlie? Isn't he staying there? And what if you mom's not home?"

"Then I'll call her on the way."

"Is she going to be surprised about us?" I try not to think of the look we're going to see on Mrs. Slater's face when she sees Tracy's.

"Don't be stupid," she says as she ducks in the car. "She's always liked you. Still asks how you are."

I can't help but smile.

TRACY'S RIGHT ABOUT her mother. She greets me with a giant hug when I enter. The joy, however, is halted the moment Tracy steps through the doorway with her battered face. She didn't want to worry her mother with it on the phone, but seeing Mrs. Slater's face now, it might've softened the blow.

"Honey, what happened?"

I'm pushed to the side as mother and daughter begin to break down with one another. They move to the living room, where Tracy tearfully recounts the horrors of her Christmas night. I sit beside her for comfort, though as she describes our morning with the police, it's clear she doesn't even need my support. Like she said this morning, she just needed to take control of the situation. Still, she rests a hand on my knee. I may not be needed right now, but I'm certainly wanted.

Tracy's phone rings, and she excuses herself to take it in the kitchen.

"Horrible. I never really took to him, but now…" Mrs. Slater nearly shakes with frustration and anger. Similar to how I was last night.

"I know," I say.

She looks up at me. "So where do you fit in with this? Are you two…?" She points her fingers together.

I nod, unsure of how she'll take it. A week ago, Tracy was merely someone that I used to know. Today, we're…I don't know exactly. We're together. That's as far as I know.

"Well," a smile spreads across her face, "it's about time."

I can't help but smile with her. How long had she been silently rooting for us to get back together? It seemed impossible for so long. I'm still surprised that this isn't just some elaborate dream.

"I wasn't sure how you'd feel after the way things ended between me and Tracy."

Mrs. Slater waves her hand in the air. "You were kids. You needed your time apart. Tracy was hell-bent on starting her music career. Nothing was going to stop her. As much as I hated to see her go, she needed to do that for herself. Besides, I could tell she still cared for you. She asked about you enough."

I look down at the floor and smile. I guess we were never too far apart. Even with everything she accomplished and experienced.

"Where do you think Charlie went?" She had told Tracy on the phone that he wasn't home.

"I don't know. He was gone last night when I got home. I figured he needed to get out of the house after they had an argument. Now I wonder if he was looking for her." Worry replaces the happiness she had just moments ago.

Tracy returns to the living room but doesn't take her

seat. "That was the police station."

"Is there a problem with your report?" I ask. "Do you have to go back down?"

"They just had a few more questions about where Charlie might be."

"Honey, why didn't you tell me you were having problems?" her mother asks.

"It wasn't this bad. We never really saw each other much. It wasn't really a marriage, now that I think of it."

"And this will be?" She waves her hand between me and Tracy.

Her cheeks flush. "So you know?"

Mrs. Slater nods.

"Are you mad?"

"Of course not." She stands to embrace her daughter. "As long as you have everything you want and you're happy, so am I."

"Thanks, Mom."

Mrs. Slater waves me over to them. "Is this thing going to work this time?"

Without hesitation, Tracy says, "I'm sure of it."

THE REST OF the day we have our own Christmas movie marathon. With the stress of the holidays behind us, and the drama of Tracy's marriage heading toward a satisfying conclusion, it's good to finally be able to relax and be lazy for a while.

After our third movie, our stomachs are rumbling, so I order a pizza. She could use the comfort food, and I don't have to expose my lack of groceries in the house. I guess that might change with someone to cook for. Better yet, cook with.

We lay tangled in each other as we wait for the food to come.

"My trainer is going to kill me when I get back to LA," she says. "I only ran once while I was here, and I've been eating like shit since."

"How long do you think you'll stick around here for?" I ask, afraid of what she'll say. Is she still planning on me coming back with her? Am I really prepared for that?

What am I thinking? Of course I am. I'm not letting her get away again.

"Well, I'm probably going to lay low for a bit. But in order to file for divorce, I have to go back to California. That's my legal residence."

"So where does that leave us?" So much for a relaxing evening.

"That's what I was going to ask you. I don't want to give up my job."

I shake my head. "I don't want that, either."

"But it's a demanding one. Not only for me, but for those in my life. If we're really going to try this again, I don't want to end up like Charlie and I did. I saw him maybe once a month. Our whole relationship was through text messages, planning the next time we'd see each other. I want this." She squeezes my hand. Her wedding ring still sits on the coffee table where she left it last night.

"What if I came on the road with you? It might help stir up inspiration for some future books. I can write anywhere."

A cautious smile sneaks across her face. "It'll be tight. We've already got plans for the tour bus. That bedroom in the back is not big."

I shake my head. "I don't care."

"And I don't plan on slowing down with this singing thing. I mean, not unless I was having a baby."

I laugh nervously. "One thing at a time."

"And the traffic in LA is horrible."

Squeezing each of her hands, I say, "I don't care. If you'll have me, I'm there."

One Year Later
Tracy

I sit on the couch and unwind the tangled Christmas lights Steve pulled out of the basement. It's been a few years since he's put them up, and I need to determine whether any of them actually work. As I untangle them, my mind wanders over the last year. Despite the relentless tabloid stories, I couldn't be happier with my decisions.

After returning to LA, I immediately filed for divorce from Charlie. By then, the police had found him at one of the hotels in town. He immediately confessed and charges were brought against him. The news had broken to the press when I canceled my New Year's Eve appearance in New York.

The divorce didn't come as a shock after that. Pictures of my battered face and Charlie's mugshot ended up on TMZ, and they went viral. Especially because I hadn't released a statement regarding the situation. Luckily, my tour rehearsals kept me busy, so I didn't face too much bombardment from the paparazzi. Still, the requests for interviews were relentless.

My phone buzzes on the coffee table, and I'm snapped out of my daydream. It's a text from Daisy letting me know she's on her way. We're supposed to meet for coffee. She wants to catch up. I haven't seen her since last Christmas.

By the time I get to Tim Horton's, she's already got a table. I wave to her before grabbing my drink and heading over.

"Oh, come here!" she pulls me into a tight hug. "My God, you're *glowing*!"

I smirk and take a seat. "A lot has happened since I was home last." Home. That's exactly what this town is.

"I know! It was all over!"

The court case that surrounded mine and Charlie's skirmish last year was big news for a month or two, especially since the divorce seemed like a surprise to the media. Charlie was slapped with a heavy fine and told to stay away from me. The end of our marriage was quick, thanks to the prenup.

I nod. "Yeah. Sorry I couldn't make the reunion this summer."

"Oh don't even! You had a lot on your plate. I took my niece to see one of your shows, and you were incredible!"

"Thank you. I'm glad you guys had fun." Despite the media attention, I plowed right into my tour, which had many sold-out shows, thanks to the publicity. Of course, I canceled all promo for the tour for the sake of my sanity—and to censor the questions ahead of time.

"The best! But besides that, tell me about your new boo." She hides her grin behind her coffee cup.

"Well, his name is Steve—"

"Oh, come on! Don't make me drag it out of you anymore. How did you guys get back together? How's it going? How did he propose?"

While Daisy leans on her wrist with a smile across her face, I recount the happy events of the last year. How Steve and I kept our relationship a secret for as long as possible, despite the rumors. How he popped the question on my birthday in May. How it wasn't easy, but we'd managed to keep the engagement quiet while we planned the wedding. In August we had a private outdoor ceremony with only our immediate family present.

"Aw, how perfect," Daisy says when I've finished. "I just remember it being all over the news when you released the statement. It was crazy."

The "news" being Access Hollywood, I'm sure.

"Try living it," I add. I had let Missy filter through the comments on social media after the news broke, and she'd only given me the highlights.

"So how long are you home for?"

"I don't really have a set schedule. Sometime after New Year's. Rehearsals for tour don't start again until the end of January, and I'm still avoiding doing interviews."

"So are you staying with your mom, then?"

I shake my head. "No, we still have Steve's place. We want a home base that's not in La La Land, and the house is a two bedroom."

"Aw, how sweet!"

"Yeah, plus he's already got his office and everything set up at this house, so he can still keep working on those books."

She takes another sip of her coffee then asks, "Any new music?"

I nod. "I'm writing a little, yeah." This whirlwind of a year is more than enough inspiration.

"Any ideas when it'll be released?"

I chuckle. "Just as soon as I can record it."

Daisy and I chitchat for a while, talking more about the reunion, which was apparently a success. I kind of wish I hadn't missed it. She shows me pictures of her kids, talks about the annoying moms of the kids in the school productions.

I allow myself to indulge in the gossip, telling her a bit about my honeymoon and the different cities I've been to on tour. In March I head overseas, which will be exciting to share with Steve.

We depart with another hug and promise to have coffee before I go back to LA. I'm having dinner with Candace after Christmas in a few days, so it'll be nice to have more than one friend back home to talk to when I need a dose of reality.

When Christmas Day rolls around, the whole family

gathers at my mother's house, like we do every year. My brother-in-law doesn't have to work, so Kimmy's here with her whole family. Tonight we're going to Steve's brother's house for dinner, but I promised my nephews that we'd be over to watch them open presents. I guess they've grown up since last year. They have a little more patience. A little.

Anything would've topped last year's Christmas, but this year seems extra special. Everyone's together, I'm completely relaxed, and I'm here with the one person I want to spend all my Christmases with.

The living room is a mess by the time the boys get done opening their presents and it's time for the adults to exchange theirs. It's hard to judge sometimes when you have money how much to spend without looking flashy and spoiling your loved ones. This year, however, I think we've nailed it.

"Steve and I have something that's for everyone," I say as I dig under the tree for the box.

"You know, if you need help finding work to pay for Christmas presents, I can get you a job at the office," my sister teases.

My mother, I can tell, would be just as happy if I hadn't brought anything. Since Steve and I got married, she's been silently admiring how happy he makes me.

"I don't think you can really put a price on this," Steve hints.

I pass the box to my mother. "Mom should open it."

She eyes me suspiciously and pulls at the ribbon.

When she opens the box, she yelps and brings a hand to her mouth.

"What?" Kimmy asks and looks over our mother's shoulder. Her eyes snap to me, then Steve, and back to the box. "Is this…?"

I nod.

She jumps up, squeals, and pulls me into a hug. My mother hugs Steve, and the boys come running in to see what the commotion is about.

The lone gift we gave to everyone this year is our first sonogram picture.

Behind the Book: *A Christmas Reunion*

I never thought I'd ever write a romance. Yet here I am at the end of my first real romance effort. Funny how things happen like that, isn't it?

When I first started this book, I thought the focus would be on the holidays. "I'm going to write a Christmas book!" My holiday short story *Snow After Christmas* was doing well, so why not try to write something similar that's a bit longer? Maybe something more grown up. So I gave it a shot and realized once I got into it that it was a different project than what I was expecting.

The idea for Tracy and Steve's broken relationship came to me while watching *Nashville*. There was a scene in the first season between Deacon and Rayna where she says something like, "I love you. That's just never not been true." That line and their awkward encounters throughout the first season is what helped me paint the picture of Tracy and Steve. Two people with a deep history, reunited many years later.

I plotted the story in about a week, wrote it over the next month, and spent collectively another month editing it, all in the spare moments of my day job. The same way I had written *Snow After Christmas*.

Working on *A Christmas Reunion* was challenging in that for the first time I was looking at not only the construct of the story and the plotting and pacing, but the dynamic between the characters. The focus wasn't on what each character was thinking as much as what they were feeling and how they conveyed those emotions. Quite different from the urban fantasy I was used to writing! No action scenes, nothing supernatural. Just two people who are drawn together.

I hope all that work has paid off and that you've enjoyed the story. Please consider leaving a review on Goodreads, Amazon, or any other retailer. Don't forget to join my mailing list to learn of my upcoming releases or sales on my books!

Thanks for reading! Merry Christmas!

It's time I found myself...

Charlotte Barlow has steadily been working her way up to her dream job at a magazine in New York City. But her success comes at a price: she's the only one single in her family, despite her mother's hope that she settle down.

Totally surrounded in your circles...

Kaden Drake might be the new guy at the magazine, but it doesn't take long for Charlotte to catch his eye. When the editor-in-chief pairs them together for a project, Kaden sees it as the perfect opportunity to ask her out. Only, Charlotte has other ideas.

Desperate to please her family for just one year, Charlotte asks Kaden to pose as her boyfriend on her trip home. Faced with another lonely Christmas, Kaden agrees. Among the decorations and home-cooked meals, it doesn't take long for feelings between them to develop. Are they real or just a product of the charade?

Available in ebook, paperback, and audio!
DavidNethBooks.com/AChristmasCharade

A chance moment. A snow storm. And the gift of a new beginning.

Tristan is ready to party and ring in the New Year by kissing his soon-to-be girlfriend, Julie. The only bad note in his rocking night is the growing snow storm. Outside his apartment, he's almost hit by Grace, the most beautiful woman with haunting green eyes. She's on her own mission to get home to her grandfather.

In a selfless act reminiscent of the age of knights and chivalry, Tristan vows to get her home...never realizing they are both on a date with destiny and their lives will be forever changed by the SNOW AFTER CHRISTMAS...

Available in ebook, paperback, and audio!
DavidNethBooks.com/SnowAfterChristmas

More by the Author

To find the rest of the author's books visit
DavidNethBooks.com/Books

Subscribe to his newsletter to be the first to know of new releases and special deals!
DavidNethBooks.com/Newsletter

If you enjoyed the book, please consider leaving a review on Goodreads or the retailer you bought it from. Reviews help potential readers determine whether they'll enjoy a book, so any comments on what you thought of the story would be very helpful!

About the Author

D. Allen is the author of the sweet small town romance series, Montana Beach and Small Town Christmas.

Also writes fantasy and superhero fiction as David Neth.

www.DavidNethBooks.com
www.facebook.com/DavidNethBooks
www.twitter.com/DavidNethBooks
www.instagram.com/dneth13

Made in the USA
Middletown, DE
01 May 2022